CW00481420

THE TAINTED SHADOW

MALEEHA KAMAL

Contact Publishing
-.-.--- -.- .- -.-.

Contact Publishing

-.-.--- -.- .- -.-.

United Kingdom

October 2005 © Maleeha Kamal

Written by Maleeha Kamal.

All rights reserved.

No portion of this book may be reproduced, stored in a retrieval system or transmitted, at any time or by any means, mechanical, electronic, photocopying, recording nor be otherwise circulated in any form of binding or cover other than that in which is published and without a similar condition being imposed on the subsequent purchaser without the prior written permission of the publisher.

The right of Maleeha Kamal to be identified as the author of this work has been asserted by her in accordance with the Copyright, Designs and Patents act 1988.

British Library Cataloguing in Publication Data.

A CIP catalogue record of this book is available from the British Library

ISBN 0-9547020-4-2

Cover Design by Rick Jones

Contact Publishing Ltd
Suite 346
176 Finchley Road
London NW3 6BT
United Kingdom

www.contact-publishing.co.uk

I Dedicate this book to:

Abbu for never giving up, no matter how distant I was
Mumma for pushing me as far as I could go
Miffoo for giving me such an opportunity
Amani who embarked on this journey with me
Ameen, the piece of heaven who ensured
I reached my destination
Samra, Safoora, Rafay for standing by
And for my grandparents who left me
with nothing but direction.

For all of you.

Love,
Momo.

Acknowledgement:

In theory there is only one person to acknowledge;
Anne, my publisher who
let this story come out the
best it could ever be.

Thanks.

AUTHORS NOTE

During the course of this novel many references have been made to prophets. I would like to assert that the following respect of 'peace be upon him' are regarded in each instance of their mention.

The Demise

The grave squeezed.
She screams, shrieks, and screeches.
It didn't work for her.
And she exhausted all three.
Exerted and Exhausted.

She tried once more. She yelped so forcefully that she thought her stinging eyes would bulge out of her mouth. Her jaw was being stretched so far that she just knew that it would crack, snap right out of place like a quill. She squealed so deafeningly that she swore her organs were rattling in her barren, blood sucked body.

She tried again.
Again and again.
Again and again and again.

Gagged and muted, her voice didn't carry further than her lips. No one heard her. Maybe they thought that she was dead. Her throat was vacuumed by the consistency of the arid lands above her. She struggled in the damp, medicated virgin white bandage wrapped around her. She was mummified for healing like preserved pickles. They must have soaked it in Zum Zum[1]. At least she would be protected from the slithering, wriggling and crawling little ones. She was sealed for transferal, surrounded by the weight and ancient, earthy odour of all that grasped her tightly in her stiff cocoon.

Man thought he had a hold over nature.
Nature waited silently for its turn in the battle.

She managed to open her eyes (which she immediately wished she hadn't because she could feel the coarse fibres of the cotton callouse her eyeballs). Her lashes dragged against her shell as she tried to determine if she could see anything. Heaven or Hell. But she couldn't. She was concealed deep in her mysterious occult, helpless and desperate like a fish wanting to jump back into its watery world.

Didn't anybody love her?
Didn't anybody need her?
Obviously, they didn't.
Was she deceiving Death, or was Death cheating her?

So she perished without any worldly love. Her spirit was spent. Her soul slid out of her like a hair out of butter. When her genuine funeral happened, she was the only witness attending the ceremony.

Her head began to feel numb, freezing into sharp, rocky ice; simultaneously the groove in the dirt seemed brighter. Drip by drip, it drained out of her. Crush. The muffled heartbeat halted deep into the distance. She was diluted.

Eventually, he came for her.
And immediately, she went.

[1] Zum Zum: holy water from Mecca

Chapter 1

'Allah Hu Akbar Allah Hu Akbar…'

The booming divulgence resonated in every corner of the dry, dusty city like a spiritual carpet, dragging and diverting directions of even those who disbelieved - for a moment. The saline air engulfed the desert; like an unfruitful, isolated woman yearning for a child, lonely and desperate for a single drop of water to breathe a life, a spirit, into her barren womb.

Life. What was life? Patience is something that you would learn in this part of the world. Even if you were the most impatient King, you would be irrevocably tamed to be quiet, tolerant and ultimately resigned. That was the brutal essence of Arabia. The geographical remoteness of the desert wastelands from nature was undefeated; the soft sand and everything that fell into the scorching sun's harsh rays was set ablaze. Water was a blessing so scarce that even sweat glistened in a thread down one's forehead before being hastily snapped up by the blazing sun. No. Faith was not a choice: it was the only way to stay mentally sound.

Close by to Aden there was a small village where mud-brick houses shaped the rugged skyline. The intense use of mud created homogeneity both in the colour and texture between the village and the ground on which it stood. It was more sculpture than architecture: the buildings just blended into the chalky mud floor, blurring any clue of distinction between them. The local suq was a colourful, lively affair with females using their very much frozen imaginations when buying items. Although men did much of the shopping, women were protected by their long black cloaks (which, unlike other colours, did not even permit a shadow to be seen) from prying gazes. Farm animals roamed freely through the village alleyways, being no different to the women who were so excitable by the items on display. They trot past professional raconteurs who enthral pedestrians with the latest news and views of the day.

'Allah Huakbar Allah Huakbar. Ashadu Allah ilaha Illullah'.

The holy call summoned again, but this time at a much faster pace. It signalled the beginning of the congregation.

Through the delicate lace worked wooden windows, all the men could be seen hurriedly covering their shops and performing wudhu[1] to get ready for prayer. Trust was not an issue in this part of the world. Everyone believed in God and, consequently, no one was worried in the least that their items would be stolen. The white pearls went towards the mosque in one direction and the black beads rolled swiftly in the other. The reverberation of their footsteps softened into a single utter. The village, the town, the city, were engrossed in a spiritual spell that Arwa felt she was a part of too.

Arwa turned away from the wooden shutters and offered her prayers. Each time she bent down to prostrate, an overwhelming sadness encapsulated her, pinning her head to the floor enticing her into being sucked in. But she lifted her head up, strongly, opposing the natural magnetism with all her force. She had become this phantom figure. Her head thrummed from making decisions upon decisions. Again and again, the naïve little girl in her would light a candle whose flame guarded her from the wispy swirls of the dark and coloured her hopes with scented illusions that would inevitably be blown out by the chilly breeze of the night.

She felt like a beaker with a hole at the bottom, sitting under a water spring.

The floorboards were streaked with aged paintwork. Clumsy blonde wood furniture was scattered about. Beneath the lip of the table chips of wood hung like teeth. A creaky bed and fresh bark peeped through the planks in the wardrobe. Everything was befuddled and deranged, rumpled like the hair on her troubled head. Arwa felt she would fit in here.

She got up and folded the rugged prayer mat away neatly. As she did so, she glimpsed at herself in the mirror. She powdered her face and applied an oily butter balm to her flaky, parched lips. Her hands glided over her fair, long neck. She caught sight of a silver handcuff gaping at her from under her sleeve. It reminded her of what her wrist should have been wearing. She dropped herself onto the frail bed which shuddered under her weight. She slid open her only drawer and took out a valuable antique jewellery box to put the handcuff away. Everything that meant anything to her was kept here, since she had been a child. This was her personal sanctuary.

A golden belly chain glimmered from within the sanctuary and shot out rays which pierced through holes in the windows, sending excitable prancing reflections on the straw ceiling. She always wanted to burn the chain into black ashes- that's what the links deserved- but her heart always prevented her from doing so. The chain was the only memory she had of her mother. Maybe Mother had been forced into it, her head told her, as it often did to justify Mother's contradictory actions. Benefit of The Doubt. That is, *if* it could be granted.

A shimmering image of Mother possessed her often. It conjured itself up in her head, pounding in with images of Mother singing and dancing, entertaining the drooling dribbles of men, including Father.

Opening her eyes back to reality she picked up a locket, the Star of David that used to be her identity. She looked at it scornfully, replacing it amongst the torn pages from children's books in Hebrew and Arabic. Over the years the pages became as soft as cloth, losing their crispness and chipped at the edges. She smiled at how Mother tried to teach her so many things. Mother had stuffed her with so much Good that when faced with Bad, she didn't know how to react. A knock at the door interrupted her thoughts.

'Syeddati Arwa. Are you ready to leave for the palace? The camels are downstairs with your escort,' came a muffled voice from behind the battered door. It was Baba, the crippled man who worked for her neighbour and landlady, Samra. He was young, yet his body was perishing away; he was kind, yet he had a hot temper.

At times Arwa had tried to understand his personality, but it had come of no use because she could never comprehend the complications of it.

'I will be there in a moment,' she replied. She put her headscarf on to open the door. She covered her face; a watcher who couldn't be watched herself.

Baba cast a sweeping glance into the tiny room. Nosiness was not a part of his nature, but this new tenant was suspicious. Her mannerisms were touching; dewy-eyed and subtle, like a child being bullied. She appeared so common, yet how was she connected to the palace? Her gait and body language revealed that she was not from the port of Aden. He looked up and noticed the box

14

on her bed. The soft, aged wood was familiar. An extreme thrilling hope overpowered him.

She walked out elegantly and straight, shutting the door behind her. Baba waited and followed her with his eyes in a mystified silence. Could it be her? Could it? It had been almost a decade. This was the only chance ever. He knew it was wrong but he just had to find out. He just had to.

He went to Syeddati Samra's, and asked for keys to Arwa's room, making an excuse that there was cleaning left to do. She was in a hypnotic state as usual, smoking opium until her brains fried, Baba felt disgusted, as he hurried back to Arwa's room. He slowly slid the key into the lock. He stopped. For years Samra had been victim to a violent marriage - and only recently she had been widowed. Instead of profiting from her freedom, only drugs healed her wounds. I should pity the woman, he said to himself.

He twisted the key and caught sight of the scattered contents of the box on the bed. He inspected the pages, the six pointed pendant and the box that only Sara, his beloved Sara would carry around with her. Rummaging some more, he confirmed his suspicions.

Doubt blurred his initial flurry, what if Arwa was not Sara, what if it was somebody else and Syeddati Arwa only had the box to keep? But, he chose to be optimistic; the little prancing fifteen year old girl he last saw was suddenly coming to life. He decided to wait until Syeddati Arwa came back- but the sensation became too great. What would Deborah say?

The empty vessel inside him which dried up into a sour powder, gave birth to a surge of emotions which had not stirred him in years.

He knew that he had to go after her to the palace.

The camels were tired. They were even slower than they normally were. Arwa mounted on the Kajawa[2] with her black dress draped on the sides of the creature like a tent. It was a long, tiring journey where she rocked gently between the furry humps. She could see the muffled figures of Bedouin Arabs swaying on the billowy dunes in the distance. They roamed the regions with their flocks and herds, seeking pasture and water from the hidden springs in the desert.

How content they seem, passing through life as if it were a one page book, being read again and again without a trace of boredom. In a way she envied their simple acceptance of life. Beggars possessed the true knowledge of this world, its tests, its traps and its temptations. They are exposed to none, but have the facts of all. Their test is emotionless, that of bare survival.

Lonely seagulls squawked quietly in the empty white sky. Arwa recalled the cobras which occasionally used to slip into the mud-brick houses back home. They would slither in, masked by the curtains of nightfall, to prowl for a bloody midnight snack. Their military attack was well sequenced: they bombarded from all directions at the same time. They roused terror in a single burst, which had the advantage of securing a definite victory. The bandits would then slip away, and lie in wait for the burial in which they would delight. But this was not the only threat to their village. Striped hyenas, bent and lurking, trespassed into the village. Although only two accounts of hyena attacks happened to Arwa's knowledge, a nightly watchman was appointed after the second report, ensuring everyone a peaceful slumber.

They finally arrived at the palace. Huge two-toned gates creaked open. Although the lifestyles of those in the palace were more advanced then hers, she felt as if she was delving into the past. Inside lay a grand structure, a symphony of slender white towers and deep golden sickles adorning the cloudless sky, placed on a splash of blinding green vegetation. Arwa's objective was simply to offer her condolences and come back. She didn't like the past. It hurt, like a sword, slicing her heart into bits. At times her heart had pumped so forcefully that she wondered if it would pound right out of her mouth. The chaperone signalled for her to mount off, and a member of the Sheikh's bevy of servants accompanied her inside to where Sheikh Khalil's condolences were being offered.

'Please wait whilst Sheikh Atif arrives.'

She looked at the grandeur, the gold of the jewels that proclaimed their preciousness in difference to every item in the room. She compared the extravagance to the dust outside the dream construction. Even the air was cooler, but artificial. The servants fanned the empty room. In the outside world no one did anything without a reason. Past the palace gates, everything was black or white. What a waste, she thought, chewing her lip.

She saw a scarf on the chair beside her. The gold coloured scarf reminded her of something. She stared at it as though she wanted to burn it, tear it to pieces with the hot needles that pinched her eyelids at the sight of it. Her hair bristled and her pupils dilated: Atif didn't want her. He didn't *need* her. He had his money to comfort him. She wanted to scream, criticise, crush everything that she could about this make-believe atmosphere so that even the white sand in the courtyard could hear how useless it was.

Everything was easier for her now.

But was it? As she waited for Sheikh Atif to arrive, she wondered how she would face him again. What would he say to her? More importantly, what would she say? Was it a mistake to come? When she had decided that she would never set foot into this fantasy again, why did she come back? She wanted to kick herself sometimes. But she was here for humanity's sake, to complete the dictates of necessity.

Death. She wondered how Atif was dealing with it. What would he know? Errors, faults and misunderstandings had steered her for the past twenty-five years. He was a pathetic living death himself. His eerie ghouls gave him comfort- he enjoyed the way they made his hair stand erect.

You can always get over the death of a person with time. It heals, she knew that for sure. But the death of a relationship, you can never get over. Ever.

[1] Ablution made prior to prayer
[2] Kajawa: Arabic word for seat

Chapter 2

The winds sliced through the date trees, as the burning sands cooled off. A thin figure skipped aimlessly in the dirt of the Jewish shanty village, on the outskirts of the city of Aden. This was Rawda Village.

The wind clung to her red dress, outlining the ripe blossoming curves of womanhood. You could see that she was not well fed as even her ribs protruded like ripples when the breeze swept by. Her brown curly hair galloped in the breeze, brushing her long slender neck which was decorated with a six pointed pendant. She had a heart shaped face, full watermelon-pink cheeks reminiscent of her baby years. Her big brown glistening eyes enhanced with long, thick flirtatious lashes. However, her small lips gave a clue to her simple subdued nature, as did her shoes. They were rugged and old, somewhat fighting to preserve her swollen feet from the times she wasted examining the dark, smelly alleyways behind their home.

The thin winter sun cast a pitiful smile onto the hearth of mud-brick houses and reed huts situated on the hilly plain. The reed huts scuttled together on the elevated edge of the area, and the mud-brick houses balanced upon the warping slopes. When the gang of winds threaded and branched out at night-time, their defence was non-existent. The reed huts were squeezed together, as if manipulated by a large invisible fist, dislodging the feeble walls into independent stalks. In contrast, the mud-brick houses only had their roofs flattened, stumped down by the log-like fingers of the same invisible hand, leaving a finger-print as a clue for the surprised villagers in the morning. In this way, the warm, dry, blistering season was much preferred. It was less of a pest.

She walked over to a shrub. Sheets of paper shuddered in its branches. They were pages from a child's book written in Hebrew with large, hand drawn pictures. Her simple mind was amused. The only thing she wished for was to be literate, like the fashionable ladies that she sometimes saw in the town when she went to sell the dolls. They walked stiff and upright, their elegant black gowns teasingly caressing their legs as they took each step. Jewellery jingled femininely, enlivening each movement. Although they spoke in husky, stiff accents there was something peculiar about them. They seemed educated, yet their husbands didn't take them seriously. But how could that be? Maybe it was her imagination carrying her into one of her thought storms again.

It was close to dusk as it dawned on her that she would be in trouble yet again with Helena, her mother. Sara did not want to cause further anxiety in her already ill mother. She picked up her dress and hastily hopped between the stones to the allotment. Busy streets clogged with traffic slowed her down.

She tried to sneak in.

'Sara, Sara. Is that you? You know I can not take care of your sister, where have you been?'

Sara's nerves tightened with the realisation that she would have to hear the nags whilst she prepared dinner. They only ate twice a day, once in the morning and once at dusk. Andrew, her father, said that it made one work harder during the day, but in reality it was because they could not afford more food. Heavily watered down soup, a fistful of rice between them, and gaining nutrition from those parts of a fish that are usually discarded was the norm. The family consoled themselves and rationalised that they were the fortunate ones.

She swept away the dust ready to lay their rationings. The powdery floor on which they all sat, slept and just about did everything was what amused her younger sister, Miriam, so much. She swayed her little palms in the dirt for ages, drawing pictures with her fingers and getting anything and everything she could find to use as her artist tools. Her tiny fingers got stiffly ingrained with dust. Everyday it was a chore washing the grime out of her hair and nails. Sara would set aside some water early in the morning especially for the task.

Sara carefully tipped the milk into five small glasses, all which were of different sizes. She then put cheap, oozing dates into an equal number of saucers. Andrew and Daud had the biggest ones since they had the largest appetites.

Helena eyed her daughter from a corner. 'No one would think that you are the eldest. All you do is waste your time in the streets, what good is there? Around every corner there is someone out there to hurt you. Why don't you listen to me? Soon I'll die and you can do what you want, but for now at least, at least for now just let me reach my grave in peace.' The suede corrugations of her cheeks trembled for a moment.

All this came out in a splurge. Sara ignored it in her adolescent way and instead she scoured the shelves for the left over pistachios from the day before. It was not that she did not feel guilty about upsetting her mother, particularly when she was so frail and withered, but she just had to go out at least once a day. She had to. She intended to take her daily ventures during Helena's naps, but sometimes, like today, she was caught. How would she react if she was informed that Sara carried out weekly expeditions to the other side of the hill, deep into the valley, searching for fresh ingredients to produce more of her natural beauty potions?

It was dangerous, Sara admitted, but she was unconvinced by the rumours of wolf and bat communities inhabiting the area. If the threat was real, someone could have claimed to sight something. No one ever did.

Sara sat in the small room which they called 'home'. What would happen to all of them if Helena really did die. How would life continue? What would happen to Mimmy and Daud? Would Father make her work more – something that Mother always strictly forbade? Her head whizzed in circles. She didn't want any of that. She would go insane like old Winona, the eerie hag who slept on the corner of Salamah alleyway, and who claimed that she had been married to an Arab Effendi. Everyone would just smile as they walked past her, knowing that the only visitor she could expect was the Angel of Death himself. Sara pitied her. She offered her any extra bit of food that the grocery stall man would give her in the souq. The hag picked at her lice and put them in her mouth as if they were Tahina[1] sweets. It was a terrifying sight, but also worthwhile when the hag's sullen face cracked a smile.

Miriam, her five-year-old sister (who everyone had nicknamed Mimmy), peered eagerly at the pistachios on the floor for their dinner. Helena said that she was exactly like Sara, but Sara could not understand how that could be. Mimmy was so wild and, well she considered herself to be calm. Maybe Helena referred to their appearances; after all, they both possessed the heart-shaped face, brown curly hair and the large eyes framed with a cluster of curling eye-lashes. Never mind, she had to lay the table before the men of the house arrived.

Helena sighed. She cast a gloomy look at her daughter quietly rubbing away at the morning's dirty plates. What a sad life. I don't know what will become of her when I leave.

It could be anytime, the Hakim[2] had warned her. She caught her reflection in the bathing water Sara had set aside to wash Mimmy. Her skin was crisp and clear, and revealed the protruding web of veins that had spun permanently onto her face. Experience washed away all the fine lines of any expressions in her, weathering it away into a plain hard sheet of ghostly grace framed with snags of black and grey hair, giving her an overall mystifying appearance. Two large sparkling eyes, hooded with sad eyelids, as if they didn't want to see life anymore, sucked in reality in its rawest form. She was a large synagogue candle, moulded before she was of any use, burnt aimlessly when she could be lit up attracting the menacing moths, until every drop of wax stripped her cold, a crumbling wick just waiting for the flame to finally extinguish.

'Mother! Mother! Look at this doll!' Mimmy dangled a doll by its leg.

'Put that away Mimmy, put it away. Sara has made them to sell,' Helena said.

Sara scowled at Mimmy to put her hard work away. What annoyed her so much was not that Mimmy played with the dolls, but that she was rough with them. Father never told her off for it either. The dolls were Sara's blood and sweat: her endless sewing, and her specks of blood from being pricked every so often by the needle. About a year ago when she began to sew, she used to yell at Mimmy, but she was firmly warned by Father who always took Mimmy's defence. Mother used to stick up for her when she was in better health. Eventually, they both gave up. Father's word was the final word, like the tolling of a bell that you couldn't ignore. The ringing would only stop only, and *if* only you obeyed his command.

Throngs of people in the market were attracted by her craftsmanship. Reed weaving boys who could not afford her dolls were enthralled by her skill. They stared longingly, throwing a glance in her direction whilst they threaded reeds together. On one occasion, Sara had given a doll away secretly to the boys, but that had been a mistake. Besides other children wanting one, Father found out. She dared not upset him again.

Mimmy immersed herself in the hulk of the greasy water. It lapped her bony waist.

'You'll catch a cold!' Sara said. She tugged the Mermaid Aspirator out in a single motion.

Mimmy floundered forward, trying to imitate a fish as Sara attempted to change her clothes.

'Hold still! Do you know that Satan's throne is in the sea? Don't become obsessed with your swimming,' she said. She was genuinely concerned that her sister would brood into the sea, and be swallowed by a great fish.

Mimmy smiled, unaffected by the threat but enlivened by the danger.

'You won't change,' Sara said. She sighed and shrugged small puddles off the reed mat.

The door creaked open, spilling in a gush of hot, salty air at them. Daud, her brother, arrived in his usual cheerful way. Sara smiled. Although he was her younger brother, he represented her whole world. He was her only friend. Daud encouraged her interest, creating youth restoring treatments from nature – by bringing some of the ingredients himself: a few oats, olives, and gram flour or sesame seeds. They shared a strange intimacy between them, teasing and playing around for ages. Mimmy envied them, wishing she could get some of Daud's attention. But it was no use. Daud lived and loved his mother and elder sister, and when he was with Sara, the world didn't matter to him.

He picked up Mimmy and started swinging her around. 'Shalom, shalom, shalom!' he sang. 'So what mischief did the Malika³ get up to today then?'

'Ssshh! You'll get Mother started again' Sara said.

'Where's the food?' he asked, as he went to greet his mother. Drops of blood followed him.

Sara bought him his plate and began to massage her brother's tired legs. Although it was mandatory in their house to wait until Andrew, their father, arrived to eat together as it was in Jewish custom, Daud made a point of stuffing his mouthfuls as quickly as possible *before* he arrived. And when Andrew arrived before Daud, Daud made out to them convincingly that he was not hungry. Hearing the growling pangs at night time, Sara would sneak in any leftovers into his blanket so he could eat.

Although Daud resembled Andrew, tall with fair skin and beady eyes, he was much thinner- Andrew even used to take things out of Sara's plate insisting that Daud needed the energy in the morning to sell the dolls, but Daud always gave it back to her later when Andrew was not around. Daud hated Andrew, the hate stiffened and sprung out at anyone if they would even mention Andrew around him. He made it a point to leave at dawn before Andrew would wake up so he wouldn't have to see his face. But Daud was Andrew's favourite. The frown lines on Daud's face soon became permanent when Andrew arrived. Sara imagined that the only reason could be that Daud knew something about Father that he didn't want to admit to himself.

This day, Daud was bitten by a dog. Stripes of blood coloured his legs. Sara and Daud quietly set about treating the wound, so as not to worry Helena. Sara stitched away at his dog bite with skill. He did not move a muscle. His mind was clogged with something strange, more concerning than the conical sand dune formation which geared itself up towards the door and blocked the entrance to the house. He was fixated on Helena's heavy anklets. They were a cylindrical horse-shoe shape, bulky and dull silver. Helena never took them off since they could only be removed by cutting with a large toothed saw. It was touching to watch her drag each foot forward as she dawdled here and there. Daud offered to cut them off, and even tried bending them off her swollen ankles, but Helena refused. She wanted to spare anyone any hassle in the numbered days she had remaining with her family.

Helena was plain, in comparison with the women customers he observed at the suq. The women he noticed wore ornaments with nose rings, bangles, pendants and wore at least one pair of studs. Why his mother was fixated upon reducing her already fading personality hurt him. She was normal, but she made herself appear abnormal and this is what bothered him. Deborah, his girlfriend, dressed up simply and was well presented. Looking at her was not accompanied with a feeling of pain, sympathy or loss.

Thump! Thump! 'Is anyone there? What do you women do in the house, sitting there all day. Is anyone theeerrrrre!'

The anger in Daud's eyes raced back with ultimate speed. Sara opened the door before the Rabbi caught Father drunk again and *they* would have to do something for the community. *They* because Father never did do his punishments. Since Daud had to work, Sara usually had to do them or even Mother. No one let their children play with them because of their father. They had no friends. A Friendless Foolish family. The last community service she did was to scrape everyone's latrines clean. Sara shuddered at how she had put her hands into the murky smelling mud-brick canisters and scooped the foul waste out. But then again, Andrew had made up for it. He had told her that she was his best daughter (she wanted to believe it, but she couldn't, recalling the pungent odours that made her loopy). He even brought her some sweets that night, without giving first choice to Daud or Mimmy, but naturally, Sara shared. Poverty didn't let one's heart consume unilaterally without sharing the delight with another.

Andrew stumbled in, wreaking of alcohol and perspiration. The corners of his shirt dripped little pink puddles on the floor, as if he had tried to erase witness-bearing stains, whilst his face was blackened with charcoal and a thick slimy layer of sweat. Andrew spent endlessly on his oblivion, alcohol- Sara never understood how he could afford it. Anyhow, she quietly gave him his plate and herself and Mimmy sat down beside him to eat. He burped. The alcohol stunk the air and ruined dinner for all of them. Andrew's face was dislikeable as it was, but when he was drunk his eyes became even more leering and slippery, making his company feel extremely uncomfortable.

Helena immediately shoved her plate away in disgust. She hated this burping, stinking drunk animal and everything that he was made of. He looked at her sheepishly. She knew what the expression symbolised. He was going to lay the snare again. To her horror, he began to tap the plates in the same rattling beat. The beat got faster and faster sending her into a trance. Pain shot through her head like darts from each side, colliding and tumbling into her already extinct chest.

He struck at the pans and plates louder and louder making her chest numb from the weight of the memories she tried so hard to forget. They contained images of her dancing and of the flowing fabrics that glided between her cushiony thighs and of the men smoking shisha[4]. Flashes. Horrible flashes.

Andrew hummed the song that he first sang when he had met her in the harem

The wretched memories crammed her throbbing head.

'No, no NO! This is *my* money *I* earned it for my children. You didn't earn a penny you middleman!'

'Shut your mouth. The only reason you have customers is because of me, my contacts. You won't get these rates elsewhere. Now give me the money!'

'No!' she screamed. 'No! You'll only drink it away. You only drink away your own wife's blood! I don't want to be a whore. You have made me into a whore.'

'You were always a whore! You hear me? ALWAYS!'

Her screams got louder and the beatings became more frequent. Helena hovered about in her married life between clouds of regret. She tried to hold her bleeding cries so that the children wouldn't hear and wake up.

Since then, the agony, the fire, the anger inside of her had built up over the brim. It was a blessing from God that she had this disease to release her from degradation, so she could spend at least some years with self-respect. She was sheltered from being the focus, their disgusting devouring eyes and gaping mouths, from their false experiences, careers and lives which they arrogantly proclaimed to be from. She was used. She was soiled in that sickly sea of sedation repeatedly. Her disease and her pain purified her. Initially, her father had abused her, then her husband. All that money could have created a better life for them, but the useless crows drunk it all away.

Of the few breaths she had left she knew she had to settle her children and keep Andrew away from Sara. Any opening he got he would throw her, bare as a meat shank in front of the ravaging monsters in the brothel. She knew once the spark of passion had been ignited, the dark sea of sedation became more and more difficult to escape from.

Daud sat spying on the ridiculous tantrum of his father in

spite. So you have even started working in broad daylight have you? You shameless swine!, he thought. Word had it that Andrew was the leader of a beggar corporation in the village. People who could find no employment or use for themselves in the world would come to him for 'salvation' to soothe their pains. Andrew fulfilled their requests, lashing away a limb or gouging an eye or two out.

To the beggars he was a pinnacle of respect, creating cripples, eunuchs and blind men. To his son, he was a menacing, uncontrollable Devil.

[1] Tahina: sesame seeds
[2] Doctor of natural healing
[3] 'Queen,' in Arabic
[4] Hubble-Bubble

Chapter 3

Sara gently closed the siddur,[1] after offering a prayer of thanks to God. She wondered if God suspected that she was sarcastically requesting things that they did not have, and she very much wanted. Mother said that Jews were meant to pray three times a day, to keep building the relationship between God and human beings and to improve the state of the heart. But Sara rarely found the time. Sewing all day long made her fingers tired and hinge-like; they hurt at the joints. That was her excuse anyway. She looked forward to the evenings when she could mix collages of spices, vegetable juices, flower nectars and fruit skins, making pastes and scrubs with which to beautify herself. Ironically, Helena was the inspiration for Sara's innovative abilities: Helena's age pointed out what had to be restored.

Threading in between columns of trees and batches of reeds, she carefully selected fresh ingredients, careful not to slip into the river. She ground, creamed and basted henna leaves and Ilb flowers to make dyes; honey and oats formed a moisturising scrub; yoghurt and lemon combined to create a cooling mask. It was her intention to become literate and write a manual of her recipes for future generations. But for the moment, she had to memorise exact quantities and combinations, listing the formulas in symbols. In recent years her ability to create successful treatments became stronger and her knack for ingredient combination perfected. Many times she attempted to treat Helena with her youth restoring remedies, but Helena was not interested. Any amount of convincing did not make a difference.

She put the siddur under the rag of a rug she used as a pillow. Tomorrow was Friday, the beginning of the Shabbat. Everyone in their family looked forward to Shabbat– even Father. Each of them felt special as they observed holy rest from the pains of practical life.

Poor, practical life

She twisted about like a wriggling worm, and glared at the smoke-smudged ceiling. The simplicity of their lives was bitter: no entertainment, no lavish meals, just hand-to-mouth. Hopefully she could marry a rich young man and have all the luxuries that she yearned for.

On one occasion she had streamed her feelings out to Uncle Mustafa, the village baker.

'Allah will reward you if you are thankful for what He has ordained you with in this world,' he had said.

It was all right for the rich to openly prescribe poverty to the poor. Uncle Mustafa, after all, used to be well off himself until he married the Jewess Shelley and his father threw him out of the family's gold business.

'Stick to your own kind,' he had advised. His large, gentle grey eyes stared into hers. She realised he had learnt the lesson himself. Rarely mentioned, Uncle Mustafa's life was a riddle in itself. The powerful lineage he had sacrificed in the name of love was of no use. His wife and children were extinguished by blazing flames in the village a few years ago. The villagers gossiped that the fire was his family's way to get their heir back, but Mustafa believed it was Fate. From that point on, he never complained about anything.

Besides, I can not just lift myself out of this life, she thought.

My surrounding buds are important to me. Mother has not long to go, and I will have to bear the responsibility of Mimmy. Daud will have to earn much more as Mimmy's appetite increases. Father, he'll be around, but in a wet, drunken presence. Liquidated and liquidising. Liquidised and liquidating.

Thoughts danced around her. She remembered the pieces of paper she had discovered that afternoon. Who would have read them? How would they have read them? And more importantly, who would have taught them to read? She slid them out from between the crevasses of the wilting rug, and carefully unfolded them. There were individual letters, with black and white pictures of little objects. It was possible to make out some of the objects. One looked like a bowl, and the other a mat of some kind. She turned the page around, so as to make sense of the objects. The bowl was actually a kippah, with a letter beside it, so it must be the sound for 'k' and the other was a tallit, so it must be the sound for 't.' Feeling very proud for solving the mystery all by herself, she let out a faint giggle, and before the next one escaped, she quickly covered her mouth with her hand. She drew the two letters with her finger in the ground, unearthing a musty smell which distinctively marked the importance of her exploration. She would practice them everyday so that she wouldn't forget.

She recalled Mother nagging, 'too much knowledge will only hurt you.' Knowledge was her future. She needed it to survive. Don't you understand that Mother? You tell grand stories of your father who, expelled from Spain, found refuge with the Ottomans. He worked in the printing presses, before you decided to leave for Yemen. If he could print, you can read. I know that, no matter how much you try to roll up the truth in the folds of your sagging illness.

Despite the fact that no one in their family could 'admittedly' read, Sara longed to be literate. She wanted to be worth more than just sewing dolls. She aspired to be like a young Helena in her glamorous clothes and shiny jewellery. Yes, she secretly wanted to dress herself up and turn into a princess, or a blooming young bride.

I wonder who will take me as his bride. Some unlucky fellow, I suppose! The thought made her hot. But, she would never tell him that she could sew - otherwise he'd work her like a dog too. She wished her mother would talk about her past life and let them in on the treasures of it. Mimmy and her could only learn from their mother's experiences and step into the shadow she tried so hard to shield them from.

The cloak of slumber nowhere near encapsulating her into its stillness and sleep, she checked to see if everyone else was sleeping. Helena was huddled into her huge white sheet- so exceedingly white that it made her seem like an illuminating phantom piled up in the corner. Daud and Andrew were adjacent, sleeping in corresponding directions. Goodness knows when Daud will grow out of his childishness, she thought, feeling like an adult all of a sudden.

My safety is in my own hands, she thought. Try and get the message. I am not a baby anymore. I am capable of making my own living. You prepared me into an adult before I developed into a child.

Her fantasy bubble popped at the faint sound of a donkey braying nearby. There was no use imagining. It was better to be realistic and accept that she would never have the opportunity of the well-off. They had opportunities upon opportunities heaped on top of each other, so many creases of bright light spilling into their lives that even the light of the sun wasn't valuable to them. What they needed was just one opportunity to show that they were just as apt, just as talented as the rich viewed themselves to be. Her legs cocked unconsciously up into the air.

Even at the tip of adulthood, Sara slept in a fetal position. It was a joke in their family. Mother even said it was almost as if she had never been born. 'Unhatched' she nick-named her. Sara tried to break the habit, trying to sleep with her legs straight and firmly pressed against the ground. At times she couldn't even manage to sleep because her quirk would bother her. She discovered to her annoyance that whenever she tried the hardest to prevent her legs from squatting in the air and her arms wrapped closely about her, somehow her thumb would *additionally* ride into her mouth. So she just gave up. It was something unique about her, a difference that set her apart from the rest.

Disillusioned, she sighed at the uneven ridges in the murky straw ceiling again. It seemed that she was destined to this clay pot forever. Tomorrow, until sunset, she would have to keep on creating different little dolls. At first, she could only make two a day. But now she could make as many as seven a day, all different individuals, wearing clothes and having hairstyles of their own. Her catalogue of imagination was based on the different women and girls who scoured the market. Since she had become so skilled, Andrew could afford to raise the prices of each one. As she created each doll, she thought about how it would be if it came to life. Like, the wild bedouin girl could live in a tent, her eyes heavily lined with kohl as she danced around the fire in the desert. The dressmaker could be hard at work everyday, skilfully using her creativity to its full extent. The princess would be a glowing pearl, delicate and fragile to everything, even her scent would be exquisite. She would be so accustomed to her rose pool baths and perfume oils so that even her breath would smell of sweet fragrance. What luxury.

Sara knew that her destiny was whatever she made of it. She wanted to save enough money (from the tit-bits she found in the street or what Daud gave her) and open a large shop with tall walls, large wooden doors, and shelves where the edges poured over with fabric trailing to the ground. She didn't want to end up like her mother. Her past was going to be different, one that she could proudly tell her children and grandchildren lurid stories about.

She peered at Helena, listening to the rusty humming noises coming out of her. Mother's loquaciousness was the loophole in her life. In actual fact, she didn't have anything to talk about. She was just a scruple, plodding through time. She liked to appear rigorous, but one glance at her wrinkles would pull her voice apart from her image like a flick. It was strange that Sara didn't know anything about her own mother. It was like living with a complete stranger. All she knew from Andrew was that Helena was a singer, a famous singer whom all the ladies in the allotment are jealous of. That's why they didn't let her play with their daughters. That's why she didn't have any friends For a moment, she was angry, but the feeling soon passed as she remembered the iron chest that Helena kept all her memories locked up in.

A pang of excitement crept through her body, making the hair on her head hum in delight. Silently, she got up and walked in search of trying to unravel the mystery behind her mother's past, *again*. Though she had seen the contents of the chest before, she wanted to touch everything, feel the silk gliding between her fingers and imagine how her mother sang. She wanted to be enchanted into the magic.

Swiftly, she made her way to the shelf where the decaying metal chest was kept. She fumbled for the key, padding around with her fingers until she found where it was. She turned the creaky lock. The lid squeaked. She picked up the oil in the bowl, and dipped the corner of her shirt in it to nourish the ancient hinges with a youthful slipperiness that they very much longed for. It was now ready. The door opened to a new dimension.

A bold bright world struck her. It was as if the fabrics wanted to be held, touched, caressed. The tiny beads and mirrors contrasted sharply with the green glittering lace. She could glimpse herself in each of the small mirrors, gift-wrapped for a queen's banquet. She dug her hands into their softness, which fondled her fingers in such a way that she could not resist the temptation they offered her. The unaccustomed luxury surrounding her sent her into paradise, woven out of her thriving fantasies. A sensational bravery overcame her. She carefully picked up two of the folded items. They were embellished delicately, with tassels hanging from all ends. One was an underwear top, but the second, well the second was a mystery. She turned it around many times to see what way it could be worn so as not to be indecent. It had transparent green slashes of fabric hanging off a very feeble belt. She put on both items on top of her own ripening body, feeling very sensual indeed. Ecstasy galloped with each heart beat.

But living in Yemen, surrounded with a culture that did not permit its women to be seen for their physicality, her cheeks blushed hotly. She rummaged around to find a veil with which to cover herself. To her surprise, she found nothing. Mother must have given the clothes away and kept the underwear, it was far too pretty to give away. Was she saving it to give to her as a present for her wedding, so that when her husband would gently unwrap her on the wedding night, as she lay numb, his heat scorching every part of her skin, she would feel special? Extra special. She stroked her entire body, a damp urge steering her into feeling the precious clothes clinging to her emerging curves.

Mimmy purred in her sleep, lying spread out like fresh laundry to dry.

It jerked Sara out of her distant illusion. She stripped off the clothing and gently shut the box with a skilful haste. She tip toed back to her rug. An unexpected thrill singed the hairs on her back, until she finally lay down to put it out. She shut her entertained eyes. This, is what the wild flower did when she thought no one was watching her.

But someone *was* staring. Staring so strongly that it was piercing the cloth that clung to Sara's timid body. He had watched the entire charade in explicit exultation; he marvelled at how the tiny shoot had developed. The flower should be picked and dispersed before it can grow thorns. Simpering slyly, he organised plans for the day ahead.

1 Siddur: Jewish prayer book

Chapter 4

In the very early morning Rawda Village was quite foggy. The mist hugged the straw roof-tops for warmth, waiting impatiently for the red disc of the sun to float up to accomplish its daily chores. Life barely stirred- the village was cloaked in a sleepy silence.

Ever so quickly, a door creaked. A young man hypnotised by the jagged course of love slid out from between the narrow crack. He has ensured that he has a valid excuse, in case he should meet any interrogation, so he takes his kippah with him as usual, crumpled up in his worn old pocket. Hopping excitedly on the vanishing murky shadows he set out, treading carefully so that the clack of his wooden soles couldn't be heard thudding against the burnt ground. He passed an unpleasant street watcher on the way.

'Shalom,' he said to the tired old man.

The day was still raw.

The handsome adolescent had gotten especially prepared for the encounter, polishing his sandals to a crystal sheen, and wearing his best green shirt. Green, Deborah said, suited him. It blended in well with the slightly bronzed sharpness on his face- although he didn't quite see the 'effect' as she described it. Clutching the handful of walnuts he had saved for her, he scurried along as fast as his legs would carry him, like a flapping leaf being tossed in the palms of the wind. He turned into main Khair Alley.

He was conscious of his appearance, his lips parted into a smile. As if attacked by the penetration of the heated stare, he halted in front of a small, detached mud-brick house. He hid in the usual shadow between the baked brown house and the three tiered apartment block.

'I'm here my darling.'

The back door opened and a young girl, clad in a red and white block print peasants gown emerged. They followed each other to the back wall of the house, silence binding them together.

They turned towards each other. His eyes drank the beauty that stood before him. She was thin, but with full rounded breasts and a slim waist, accentuating her slopes further. Thick coils of ebony hair surrounded her deep green eyes.

'I missed you so much,' she whispered. She leaned into him.

'Now Deborah, please control yourself, we do not want to create a scandal now do we?'

'Daud! No one knows we are here.' She cuddled up closely into him, moulding herself into his body. A thin layer of prickly tingles simmered between the two immature bodies.

He kissed her on the forehead. An urge crackled between them. Embarrassed, he changed the topic and took out the walnuts he had brought for her. She accepted them graciously.

'How is your mother?' he asked. Stimulating a conversation, to avoid passing hour after hour without exchanging a word as usual.

She looked up at him. 'She's just fine. Just making the usual matches- she is really overloaded with requests at the moment.' Her foster mother, Monica, was the village matchmaker, and was considered as valuable an asset as the fortuneteller to the village. Many successful weddings were the result of her knack for setting compatible people up. 'Let's talk about something else,' she said. She pressed herself into him.

Her forwardness was extremely flattering, but sometimes Daud felt humiliated. 'Deborah, my dear sister, we are not married, so kindly control yourself.'

She didn't like hearing the 'dear sister,' despite knowing that she was three years older than him. She drew herself away.

'We shouldn't even be holding hands. Our will power has cracked beneath us, let's not allow it to split any further.' Although ironically, she was saying this to Daud, she was actually speaking out loud to herself. She often did this. It's funny how man always wants to taste the forbidden fruit.

Torn between fascination and a religious moral code, she hunted for something to prevent themselves from flinging into another passionate embrace. 'Oh yes, I have some fresh news for you sweet heart. Helena visited us a few days back.'

'Mother?' He clenched his fingers together. 'Whatever for?'

'Oh well, she only found out about us,' she said.

He took her hand and pulled her into himself. 'So how did she manage that?' He stroked her neatly combed hair. Today it smelt of fresh jasmine. She had fragranced it especially for him. The authority of him in her affections sent him into elation.

'Well she did come,' she said, 'but not for us. She was extremely worried about Sara. Wanted to get her married soon.'

The misery of reality that deserted him for a moment came hurtling back in his direction at full speed. 'It would be better if she got married. That way at least she would be settled,' he said.

'Then we could get married!' she said.

'Sssh! Yes we can, Deborah, but after some time. Her wedding will cost me a lot. Father will not pay for anything, no matter how many beggars he lines up. My sister's wedding will be lawful.'

'I understand.'

Overcome with guilt at stating the obvious, his eyes latched onto the depression in her eyes. He raised her face to his, and they exchanged a long, pressing kiss. The forbidden fruit was juicier than ever.

Helena left the allotment in the early hours of the morning to visit the Hakim.[1] She rarely stepped out of their home for any other reason. Recently, the pain had become too much for her. So much, that she could feel the unearthly stillness that hovered sheepishly around her aching limbs. She took small steps, one at a time, as she wended her way through passer-bys. Her eyes focused on the floor, making her movements appear somewhat shadowy and guilt-ridden. Her coarse feet were thin, but muscular despite her illness At least there was one advantage of that wretched life. Every so often she would worry about Sara and Mimmy, but Sara more. Her death was creeping up on her, and though Mimmy had protection, she knew Sara didn't. Andrew would cunningly deceive Daud for his own means. This world was made for the male. Everything about it suffocated out the female carrier, the mindless baby producers. Women were factories, men were the owners. The food she cooked was dictated by him, the clothes she wore was to satisfy his requirements. Even if a woman acted modest, it was a façade to make herself appear decent and inexperienced. A woman was forced to retain and treasure her femininity. 'Submission,' was a more fitting word, she thought.

She increased the frequency of her steps. The horse shoe anklets collided with her ankle bones. Once the soil is seeded, it never feels quite the same. The same desire, the same purity does not embrace a virgin twice. She kept her anklets on to draw weight, to restore a balance and to prevent her spirit from soaring up high into the sky.

A black remainder of a bonfire reminded her that they must re-stock their wood. They could not afford fuel from the timber market, so Daud made a pact with the village boys: he helped them trawl for their breakfast in the river, and they assisted him in carrying remnants of felled logs to their home. She would ask Daud as soon as she got back.

Her eyes sought the Hakim's room, hoping the usual hoards of Bedouin patients were not there to greet her. The scorching heat tired her out. She saw it and stepped in, ringing the bell to indicate to him that he had a patient. The room was familiar to her, filled with bottles of herbs, spices and multi coloured powders. She stared at the vessels littered with medicines and his ingredients, as she wondered in melancholy at what she would be prescribed this time. And more importantly, whether she could afford it. Poor Daud, she thought as she waited for the Hakim to arrive he was so responsible, sweating for his sisters and mother. Unlike his father, the black crow, who only plunged himself deeper and deeper into Hell. But she didn't care. She had stopped caring the day they got married. He didn't ever love her and she didn't love him. She was more than aware that she was nothing but a morgue to him, and he was nothing but a conniving, blood sucking leech to her. It was a business investment from the first night onwards- for the both of them. However, his venture succeeded and demolished hers.

'Assalamo Alaikum Syeddati Helena, are you worried?' the Hakim said. He noticed the painful scowl slapped across her face.

He was a middle-aged red-faced man, who had an enchanting glow about him. Everyone respected him for his knowledge and the successes of his treatments. Once you were diagnosed by him, you would never complain again. He possessed a wizard like talent which granted him his reputation. Helena longed for Monica, the village match maker to be able to find a hard working husband for Sara, with a good salary and a high social standing as the Hakim.

'Wa-alaikum Assalam' she replied. Her face was discoloured, owing to the nature of her thoughts. 'Well, yes,' she began, steering the topic to the reason of her visit 'my pain has increased and my stomach keeps filling with water. Sometimes I can't lie down because the water gushes to my mouth, so I have to stay sitting up.'

He nodded with sympathy. He must be quite used to having that sorrowful expression look on his face. Maybe he should make it permanent, Helena assessed pessimistically, even though his compassion never ceased to touch her warmly. Sarcasm swooped around her like a shawl since life had betrayed her.

'I will give you a liquid syrup to ease your pain. You may feel a little tired, sedated and sleepy. But sleep is good for you. Get plenty of rest.' He held her gaze for a moment.

She looked away. 'Will it be a honey-based syrup?' she asked nervously, knowing that despite the benefits, honey was extremely expensive. She had rejected its prescription twice already.

'Yes, but this time I will not let you leave without it. Consider it a gift,' he said.

She could feel the black spikes of his gums dig into her. She despised his smile that revealed his yellowing fangs. 'No, how can that be?'

'Trust me, Helena. You have visited me for years, and I want you to take it,' he said. He mixed and shook different powders and liquids into the pot above the fire as if he were a magician, brewing a spell of some sort.

He reminded her of Sara, mixing pastes and potions to restore a permanent life. Sara restored a permanent beauty. Both didn't exist.

'Come here, you must take this,' he said.

'But I simply can not,' she said. This wasn't the first time he had given her treatments for free. She stared at the colourful geometric patterns on the rug underneath her in guilt. Tiny globules of dust and sand seated themselves between the intersecting fibres.

He handed the glossy tin bottle to her, their hands brushing against one another, his soundly wanting to clasp hers tightly. His face clouded over in an instant, and he turned towards the wall to pick up a bag for her.

'Shukran,' she said. She left the money that she had with her on the floor. Helena got up, pulled her veil tightly around her and began to walk away.

'Visit me again tomorrow if you find no relief,' the Hakim yelled after her.

1 Doctor of natural healing

Exit and Re-entry

Arwa's grave was hospitable after she recovered from the initial trauma that she was buried alive in it. The walls were decorated with her deeds, wide airy and pastel coloured. The grave cubicle next to hers was uncomfortable. She knew this because she heard the body knot and wriggle in the uncomfortable space allocated to it, suffocating under each defeated struggle.

Her soul escaped!

Arwa followed her exit out of the world beneath his towering cloak, and skimmed past the palace courtyard. There stood her traitor, agonising over the iniquity which barged into them from all sides. A thin hand scratched a plump leg. Skin crawled over skin, itchy and infested. Lice upon Louse.

She turned away, back into the parachuting cloak which soared high into the skies. She felt her face mould itself without it moving. Everything held its own account. Unsure whether the particular knowledge of her traitor's Fate soothed her or twanged her, she could only confirm that she didn't care anymore.

Not for anything. Not for anyone.

Chapter 5

Andrew staggered out of his sleep, waking up later than usual. He assessed that the house was empty and pulled out his crumpled up treasure, his prize for living with such a pale deadly woman who gave him no pleasure. He began to disassociate himself as he lit the scarce straggles of opium that he had stolen from the watcher man on one of the trade ships. He tossed the stubby match outside the door, he fell back against the wall, and bubbled in ecstasy.

In the past few days he had been seeing Cynthia, the woman who had saved him from poverty when he was a little boy. She was like his mother, and had even introduced him to Helena, his cursed wife. What she used to be and what she had decayed into, he chuckled to himself. He yelped out like a stray dog at the smoke that he was shelled in. He thought about Cynthia, his mother, his friend and who now was his lover. It was funny how one person could fulfil so many roles. It was of no interest to him that she was years older than he was. He just needed the facility, the tranquillity to ooze his reality out of him every so often. Besides, he found her attractive enough to stir his emotions. What mattered was that she was *daring*. Daring enough to think of new short cuts so that his pockets would swell with coins upon coin for a few days (it would last longer but for his lavish spending habits). And when his pouch was empty she would conjure up a fresh new scheme. She was dangerously wonderful. he thought, blood speeding through his veins as he realized that he needed to visit her again.

He snubbed the flame out of the crackling roll of paper. Walking up to the bucket of water, he washed his face and smoothened his hair with his stubby fingers. He washed himself down but found no need to change his shirt, which was damp with perspirations of all kinds. He perfumed himself with some drops of rose water realising, hoping that it would mask the smell of his own rotting juices. Cynthia won't mind. She never did. 'After all, I must be better than some that she has been with,' he chuckled out loud. He began to make his way to her shack at the corner of the hill. Erotic passion infused his veins with a sizzling ardour which he felt tingling even the tiniest hairs on his body.

The trunk of a tree bent madly over to one side. It brushed the top of her shack.

The warmth rolled in his chest as he knocked on the feeble door. He put a qat leaf in his mouth for an image of stylistic virility. 'Cynthia, you there? I've come to visit you my darling.' He walked straight into the bedroom.

Cynthia lay on the bed, resting herself on the back of her wall, seductively draped in nothing but loose sheets, her black hair flowing onto her shoulders. She was an older woman, notably older than Andrew but extremely sensuous and clingy in her appeal.

'You're here Andrew,' she said.

'Couldn't keep myself away.' He smiled, revealing the uneven gaps in his teeth as he flopped down on the bed beside her exposed supple olive thighs.

She ruffled up the sheet around her. 'What brought you here apart from my love?' she asked, knowing very well that Andrew was troubled by something other than to simply vent out his lust.

After a short pause, he blurted out, as if wailing about a bully, 'I need money Cynthia. I need money, Helena is no use as you know, Sara and Daud earn, but what can I do? I need to eat and sleep in peace.'

'Well. I have already given you some of the items my customers give me to sell. We do not have any girls to work for us anymore. The damned Arabs are so tight that they always find out when some girl is kidnapped.' She grit her teeth so fiercely that her lips almost turned blue.

'Hell. Don't know why. They act as if their forefathers never kept concubines for their pleasure,' Andrew muttered, cutting her off as he plopped his head in her lap. 'Hypocrites.'

'Listen Andrew,' she said, 'this is our rebellion against the rich. Whatever we do is because of the differences in classes. If we are dressed in rags, it is because of them, if we have food in our houses we owe it to them. They are our neighbours, but they don't care about us. If I am a prostitute, it is due to them. If you have to go around doing extreme make-up for 'beggars' it is because of them. In this way we create a revolution against them, enticing the Creators into their self-inflicted corruption.'

'I remember, I remember,' Andrew repeated, bored, recalling all the teachings his foster mother had taught him. The world will always revolve around the rich, whilst Time will only encircle us. Our theatre is for them, the prosperous audience, to find a heart and reward us.'

Cynthia gazed at him, with the love vibes charging out of her as usual. She was proud of the entrepreneurial skills that she had passed onto Andrew. He lashed out at the world that had denied her redemption. She hated all the rich. A rich man had molested her whilst her mother had watched terror stricken. She was hushed for a heavy wallet of money. It was then she had realised this was the cheat's way to get easy money. However, she genuinely cared about Andrew, he was her only attachment to the world.

The problem was you could never tell if she was talking to him as a lover, son, or a gangster. It was a mystery to all. Sometimes even Andrew got confused.

'It's alright for me,' she said. 'At the end of the day I will always have myself to sell, I can maintain a reasonable lifestyle. But Andrew, you really should get yourself a decent job. You have children to take care of.'

'I know,' he replied. He dug his greasy face into her firm, shapely bosom. 'But I am not disciplined. Those small jobs pay you nothing, and you sit there all day working like a donkey,' he mumbled out from between her rounded breasts. It was a well known part of his character that he was a vagabond. Lazy, useless and strangely rebellious.

She stroked his hair. Her eyes glinted at the idea that had been festering in her mind since Andrew had set foot in the shack. 'A man did visit me yesterday. He buys girls to sell them as maids in the house of the more affluent Arabs. The Arabs do not let their girls out without a chaperone, so they need maidens for them. The trading takes place mostly in Sana…' She paused. 'What about Sara? You would make enough money so as not to have to work for at least two years. He makes the travelling arrangements himself.'

'Yes I could. Couldn't I? I was thinking of using her somehow anyway. I never had a fondness for Sara. She'd leave the rest of us in peace and luxury. Including you, my dear,' he said, turning her face to his. The tint of greed reappeared in his eye like a signalling flag.

The sweat that trickled around the paths that two scratches had carved on his face alarmed her. One was short and quick, the other was meandering, as if purposefully engraved to signify something, Whoops of children would run away from this monstrous man.

'Come over here,' she said, 'don't forget what you came here for first!'

'I will not pay more than three ducats,' Daud stated quite adamantly to the honey seller.

'But it is worth three. Tell me why should I give it to you for less? Where is the profit for me then?' Honey was a rarity, a divine luxury that only came to the village suqs at fortnightly intervals.

Daud dug into his pocket, knowing that there was enough money there, but he wanted to save that for other medicines that his mother might have required. He paid the stubborn salesman and took the small jar. It was so small that it could fit into the palm of his hand. He recalled how, a month back, he had waited outside the Hakim's room for Helena to return, and was very upset to hear how she had turned it down because of the price. Since then he had been relentlessly saving to buy her some honey. Deeply absorbed in reflections, he made his way home.

His train of thought came to a halt as he saw Andrew's face amongst those bustling in the crowds. Daud knew very well where he had spent the morning and how he would claim he had been 'working.' In reality, the only work he did was sell his daughter's hand made dolls. Daud gritted his teeth as he watched him chew qat, a local narcotic which his father's teeth were usually stained with. The ease and laziness of how his mouth went round and round with his black tongue rolling around in enlarging circles, agitated Daud even further. In his fury he did not notice the two boys walking in front of him. He butted straight into them in his vicious haste. All three of them toppled over one another in the middle of the traffic, clogging the street.

Daud stared up at them. They were Elijah and Ethan, neighbours in their hilly plain. Normally Daud avoided them, since he found them quite odd. *Effeminate* was the word.

'I apologise, my head was just wavering without me,' Daud said. He emptied the sand out of his sandals.

'Don't you worry. It happens to the best of us,' Elijah replied. 'I suppose it was because you saw Andrew here was it not?' He flapped his long eyelashes on his soft creamy face. It was unpleasantly evident that he paid special attention to the texture and tone of his face.

Aware that everyone in the village knew that he had no relationship or respect for his father, he nodded with guilt.

Ethan just stood there, silent, like a vain stork, hips sticking out to one side, tossing the long blonde locks off his face. Why these two young men wanted to look like neuters was far beyond Daud's understanding. Men should look like males: smelly, rough, sweaty. What use was it being a man if he resembled a female? These two were truly an animated pair of eunuchs or something of the ilk. May God forgive him for thinking this way, but he couldn't help it. It was as if the pair were created to provoke the watchers' opinions. It was a purposeful plan on their part.

Noticing the curious expressions on his face, both Ethan and Elijah bade Daud farewell, as if wanting to avoid the vexation that could follow if they stayed. Daud shot a glance in Andrew's direction. 'Where were you dear Father, in your foster mother's lap or crippling yet another 'beggar'?' he fumed sarcastically in a fierce whisper, 'I hate you. I hate you more everyday. If it were up to me I would kill you with my own hands…'

Andrew was busy buying some small, hairy mangoes. 'Of

course, it's the Shabbat today, how could I have forgotten!' he said, out loud. He weaved his way through the gaps in the cloth of people in the market. It was tiring, since there were a lot of them about after their Jum'ah prayer. Bedouins were seen bargaining with the sellers, their primitive tribal squeals silencing those immediately around them. He raced home at top speed, wanting to reach home before Andrew did, wrecking the Shabbat for them all.

'My father, the human butcher,' he cussed, turning into a short cut which would ensure his arrival before his father's.

He had stumbled upon the discovery of his father's reality by coincidence when he was rushing to the Hakim's to get Helena's medicine one night. When he turned back towards their home, he saw Andrew in the distance negotiating with two men. He was touching them as if he was assessing the ripeness of a piece of fruit. He crouched in between the wall of the baker's and the barber's shops with the stray cats. The cats got bored of licking themselves, so began to smother a fishy, greasy film on Daud's exposed legs. They painted his legs in stripes of cat saliva. It was sickening, but the spy was preoccupied with this new mission. He watched on as Andrew hauled out a few bricks from the wall. The men went in, one after the other, scared, but with an obvious excitement on their faces. Rip roaring screams resonated into the thickness of the night, until they finally came out. One was limping, the other was moaning with pain as he held the limping one for support.

'Shukran,' they stammered to Andrew. They went in the opposite direction. Daud crept towards the secret wall. The red glows of rats' eyes were visible in beady pairs riddling the place like an epidemic. He lit the candle that he carried with him all the time for guidance. The scene was horrifying.

Arms, legs, and feet were piled all over the floor, dripping in a rotting coat of blood. His own eyes almost fell out into the heap at the haunting sight. Rats squeaked, slurping up the fresh blood. Daud quickly replaced the bricks, unable to contain his terror. He tried to run back home, but he fainted.

At Fajr, Uncle Mustafa found him lying like a rag in the street. Uncle Mustafa was a pious man, whose faith healed him of his life's sorrows. 'My dear son, are you alright?' he asked.

Daud woke up from the strangling claws of his nightmare. 'My father! My father. Oh you don't know! Why?' he shrieked, gritting his teeth and sprinted back home as if all the limbs were chasing him in a frenzy.

Uncle Mustafa watched him flee into the distance.

'My poor son,' he shook his head knowingly with genuine concern. 'Allah please let his awakening be gentle.'

He turned back towards the mosque to pray some more.

Chapter 6

The steady serenity was soon broken when Andrew arrived. Sara, Mimmy and Helena were all 'resting' in the pink oasis of calm provided by the long bent candles that Sara had placed around the room. They had two short fat ones that were not bent, but looked as if they had been squashed between bricks as the wax formed uneven ripples on the edges. Mimmy waved her fingers through the thin, lengthy flames, feeling quite agitated at the placidity that prevailed at the moment. From a distance she looked quite eerie and mad, the excitable expressions on her face highlighted by the beige glow from the candles.

Daud left the door ajar, so that no one would have to get up and make an effort for Andrew. No one should have to do anything to make that mongrel feel honourable. Andrew hopped in, ecstatic with the plan that was already in full motion. 'Shalom! My family! Look what goods I have brought for you all to devour and remember!' he exclaimed proudly. He dragged in a casket that bulged with fruits and vegetables.

Their jaws dropped open like water cascading from the edge of a waterfall. The sight and smell of so much food gnawed their barren nostrils which were not accustomed to seeing such a large quantity that *they* could consume by themselves. Dates, oranges, khoubz, papaya, parsley and large bundles of pulses were compressed in the withering old casket. Andrew smirked quietly to himself at the sight of their bewilderment. Their eyes visibly ogled at the food in cones, wanting to scoop it into their dry mouths.

All of them were under a genie's spell: the magnitude of the shock did not allow a single squeak to escape their lips. Mimmy was the first to break the silence.

'Father, can we eat *all* that food?' She plopped a handful of oranges and dates into her lap.

'Of course my dear. But that is not all I got you. I have a present for each one of you to make up for the times I have returned home drunk and senseless,' he replied, as he hauled in a rugged brown bundle from behind the door.

Everyone watched on, not knowing what to expect next. He untied the ruddy bundle to reveal three colourful fabrics and a light blue checked one in a smaller bundle. Andrew handed the smaller bundle to Daud, who almost dropped it on the floor. Andrew pretended not to notice and continued to entertain the rest of his spectators. He handed the saffron coloured fabric to Helena, a small piece of minty green to Mimmy, and a ripe, red scarlet material to Sara.

Sara, nuzzling her present, drew her fingers between the folds in the fabric, to sense its thickness. She was amazed to find that she could see the edges of her fingers and the milky crowns of her nails, even in the dull candlelight. The sensuous way the fabric embraced her hand reminded her of Helena's chest, which spewed with provocative underwear.

'Thank you Father, but where ever did you–'

'Andrew!' Helena had been watching the entire episode mutely from her corner. 'Tell me where did you steal all of–' She saw her children staring at her. 'I mean, where did you manage to get all of this from?'

She demanded this from him in a strange combination of authority and disappointed eyes, knowing very well that he must have committed one crime or another to be able to bring such luxury in a single burst into the house. Even Daud was familiar with the fact that his father whose pockets were empty and filled with nothing but ruddy ashes from his smoke, must have had to do something quite outrageous to spend so lavishly. He knew too well that Andrew would not have sacrificed his obsessive addictions to treat them to such a generous glory. No, all of this was brought with *extra* money.

He gently nudged Sara to begin laying out the food onto the floor. 'I had been saving it for many months now. I wanted to treat you all to a feast that you would remember.'

Lying came to him as easily as breathing. It just stuck itself onto him. In actual fact, after the breathtaking coupling session with Cynthia he had slyly slipped off one of her gold rings and later sold it in the market for an abundant sum. A large amount of which still remained in his pocket. He'd return it to her once his plan blossomed.

'Come on. It's our Sabbath today. Our family day. You might as well enjoy it whilst it's all here. A week from now you will be kicking yourselves for not making use of it whilst it was laid out in front of you,' he said.

Eventually, they gave in to the gnawing temptation that was spread before them. They attacked it from all directions. Helena was the only one who refused. She mourned for the poor soul that would be at major loss from eating the food. She wished she could have stopped her children from consuming unlawful things. But, her growling stomach eventually gave her away to everyone in the room, and she surrendered.

Later, she was glad that she had.

The evening deepened, swelling the sky with a spray of glimmering diamonds, varying in their sparkles like newly hatched tadpoles that bobbled up and down at the surface for air. Andrew stood leaning against the open door of the allotment, staring at the sky whilst everybody else was getting ready to go to bed. He inspected them scattered randomly on the ground. The food had made them quite plump and sedated, since their usually vacant stomachs were not accustomed to such a heavy load. An enlarged bump grew out of them all.

Taking care not to lose sight of his intentions, he silently took out a little packet he had brought from the Hakim for insomnia. 'Instant sleep' is what he had claimed. 'My eyes are red and patterned with veins,' he had said.

The Hakim jeered at his theatrical skills.

'Honestly, you are almost as convincing as a woman who makes excuses not to make love with her husband anymore! I hope your plan works,' he sneered, revealing the black silhouette which outlined his spiky teeth in elongated shapes. 'Fifty, fifty,' he reminded Andrew, thrusting the drug into his palm.

'Don't you worry my friend, this partnership will reward us both.'

Their partnership had come about when the Hakim could not find cures for some conditions. He found that long-term medicines that he prescribed were more costly than a lump sum fee. So he approached the renowned Beggar King, and they agreed that incurable patients were better off disabled.

This devious trade between the two was considered by both as beneficial to society. They actually thought they were doing others a favour. They gave them a reason to live. At least this way they could earn at the same time as being unhealthy. So what! Now they were a little more weak, but it would support them. That was their motto.

He squeezed the leather pouch that contained the strong odour of cloves and peppermint in his pocket. He made his way to the corner of the room where Sara cooked flat bread. He lit a peach flame, the plumes of which spiralled dangerously in the dark, turning into a deep purple as the flame heightened. Next, he filled the largest pot with the fresh milk, adding sugar, crushed pistachios, coconut and cardamom pods. It brewed gently until it foamed into a hot, creamy sweet smelling version of Hareera. He poured the mixture into four goblets. He sprinkled the drug into the first three. The roasted nut aroma capered around the room.

Mimmy furthered his plot without any effort on his part. 'Father,' she said, 'Can I have some milk? And is that for everyone else? Shall I give it to them?' Her voice was shrill with excitement at the hot nutty, creamy drink that stood by her feet.

This had woken everybody up although, in stubbornness, they had tried to block out the aroma seeping up their nostrils and into the pores of their sun-blasted skins. They eagerly accepted their milk, even Helena, whom Andrew was convinced could have sabotaged his map of mendacity. He rejoiced at how effortlessly they were falling into his trap.

Sara drank from the goblet which did not contain the drug.

Andrew gurgled down his milk portion in an animal-like slobber, and lay his head down to pretend that he was asleep. However, his hands kept fidgeting in restlessness, like a fat fish on its belly wriggling to get back to the sea. But no one noticed this. Neither did they notice the leering and slippery eyes sparkle with pride in anticipation of their next shadowy movement.

During the night, Sara lay awake on her rugged mat as usual. She was not wide awake, but was overcome by that feeling of simultaneous restlessness and tiredness that doesn't grant one peace to go to sleep. She tossed over to her right side, heaving her expanded belly that felt as if it had a brick inside it. This is how it felt like to be pregnant. The voluptuous mangoes swelled with their bitter-sweet juices, the creamy papaya and the soft, oozing, dates. She wanted to be able to tantalise her taste buds once more, so she swept her soft, rouge tongue in between the fold of her mouth.

Excitement brewed inside of Andrew. He faked a few muffled coughs to ensure no one would stir in reaction. To his delight, only Sara reacted by twitching her eyelashes in response to the sound. Step three was now ready to take place.

He began to lose sight of what he was supposed to do under Sara's steady gaze on him. She knew that he was wide awake, and he would be sure to make use of it. Andrew was not capable of many things, but he was the only Jew in their community who could make a false impression so realistic that even *he* would forget that he was faking it. Maybe he *was* as convincing as a frigid woman! He looked for a vessel with which to drink water. He padded his hands down everywhere and anywhere like a blind person.

'Sara, Sara are you awake? I need to find a vessel to drink water. Water I tell you, my throat is very dry.' He let out dry, itchy vocal sounds.

Sara got up cautiously, to avoid tripping over Daud. He was sleeping spread out, like a hardened starfish, his lips twitching in a sucking motion as if he was suckling milk from his mother's breast. She poured the water and gave it to Andrew, who was excessively grateful for it. He took it from her outstretched hands, purposefully letting it trickle out beyond the rim of the vessel and onto the edge of his jaw, like raindrops. Sara appreciated how well he had treated them that evening.

He grappled at the opening and made his way towards the window. He fished out some glistening green bangles from behind the cover on the sill, and smiled as he twirled them in the starlight suspecting that Sara might come up to him. She did.

'Are those for Mother?'

'No, they are for you my dear. I didn't want to give them to you in front of Mimmy, you know how upset she can get at times.'

'Are they for me! Really? This was the first kind gesture Father had made towards her without bartering her for anything else. She felt their smoothness on the edge of her fingertips, circling their fragility. Their fluorescent glow threw itself in all directions.

'You want to go for a walk Sara?' Andrew watched her slip them onto her delicate feminine wrists. 'My, they do look spectacular on your hands don't they.'

'Thank you Father.' Her cheeks blushed visibly into a cherry red. She bent down to kiss him on his forehead. Andrew felt a cold sludge jolt inside of him, but he shrugged it off. He pulled away almost immediately, startling Sara.

'Sara dear, do you want to come with me for a walk? A beautiful adventure in this beautiful night?'

She agreed. She had been tired of ploughing for his affection, and took this easy route to bore a permanent hole of attachment for herself. But then she hesitated. Her action would upset Mother, who always told her to keep her distance from her father. She felt pressured into an uncomfortable position. Her face crumbled into a layer of panic on the floor.

'We'll be back before they wake up,' he said 'Don't you want to go for an adventure? See the camels- even ride them?'

For a moment, she was swayed. 'But Mother...they won't find out will they?' She hoped it would remain a secret between father and daughter.

'It'll remain a midnight travelling experience for the both of us,' he said, 'And you don't want to take anything with you do you? We'll have a special dessert on the dunes and you can tell me about it.'

It was a strange question, but then Sara contemplated that perhaps he was asking her so that they would have something to talk about on the dunes. She decided to share her most prized possession, her life's glory: the antique jewellery box that Helena had given her on her Barmitzfah.

She slipped on her sandals. Sara shredded away the maternal shield that always sheltered her, piercing it to threads as she followed Andrew into the cold, breezy night.

Baby bird under eagle's eye.

Mimmy yawned. She recognised the sound of the sandy friction of the grains that scrubbed between the dry floor and their sandals. She went to see where they were going, *without her.* She put on her little mules and decided she would catch up with them.

On the way, she passed an eerie white puddle that glowed luminously in nature's light. It was her milk, which she had tipped outside the window when no one was looking. It didn't taste quite as nice. It smelt like raw egg-white now, with oily globules swimming in it. Without hesitation, she kicked some earth over it and scampered eagerly behind Sara and Andrew.

Chapter 7

The air evolved into a thick salty mist as they progressed further south. It hooded them like a jilbab, covering them all over. The ground was dotted with random weedy vegetation, giving it a springy property.

Sara plodded along, wondering how much longer they would have to walk. She tried to keep up with Andrew's pace. 'Father, why are we walking so fast?' she huffed under her heavy breath, trying to prevent her bangles and jewelry box from clinking together. 'Father, if we race any more, my bangles will break!'

Andrew stopped and glared at her with such solidity that she was convinced that she would shatter into pieces. But his hardness, (thankfully) melted away like soft wax and he cushioned his arm intimately around her shoulder. 'Sara if we don't hurry we'll miss our chance to mount the best camels. Besides, we need to get back home before everyone wakes up and gets worried why we are not there. It's my fault. I should have at least informed Daud before we left,' he said. He pulled the most pity worthy face he could. His face possessed a clay-like quality, which he moulded into any expression he desired, sliding into any mood to fit any situation.

Sara nodded and followed, hopping like a frog, lily to lily, somewhat confused. Dust sprinkled onto them like seasoning as the breeze blew harder, and they found that they were entering a midnight suq at the edge of the desert plain. The Mystic East: dark leathery tents, large illuminating lanterns which threw their glows on passers faces giving them a yellowish zesty charm, colourful red and black Bedouin striped floor seating on the ground…and saturated with males. Absolutely swelling with men who had stiff pointy beards and thick leathery skins. Some were busy bargaining and trading with each other and others, clearly overfed, lazily smoked shisha while gulping down miniature cups of mint tea. The slapping down of playing cards kept a monotonous clicking sound in the air. This was more bearable than the clamour of the daily suq. It was nice to have a cool watery breeze breathing on you consistently, Sara concluded. Women were exempt from the testosterone saturated air, Sara apparently was the only one present. And all eyes, naturally, were focused on her. She felt handfuls of penetrating stares stroking the smooth curves of her body.

The coastal drift attacked. Blades of grass screamed, flinging themselves on the earth as the wind raped them. The grass whined, the drift panted.

Andrew tugged her arm, interrupting her observation. 'This way,' he said. 'You want to see where the ladies are kept?'

Kept? What ever does that mean? Just as she saw prowling eyes focus on her antique jewelry box, her thoughts cluttered into a messy pile at the back of her head. She pulled her scarf over it and pursued in quick footsteps after Andrew.

To her dismay, he led her to a long line of camels. Ah. So that's what he must have been referring to.

The gust was blustery, making her curly locks flap fiercely around her face. The gold and white creatures stood tall and patiently, chewing from what their masters gave them. Some had their skins charred in charcoal black near the tail, which looked quite peculiar. Sara deduced that this was probably because they were too old and were going to be consumed as camel meat. She wavered between their tall legs which stood like pillars of a luxury cage around her. 'So *you* are the baby,' she said as she fondled the chin of a young white camel sucking milk from its mother's udder. The camels fluttered their lustrous long lashes at the young girl.

She stared at the baby camel, which was staring just as inquisitively back at her, when Sara felt a chill down the small of her back. It wasn't the usual kind of chill she felt when she was being told off by Helena. It was a sweaty chill, freezing; yet she noticed the single droplet of sweat wriggling down her spine.

Your innocence is what attracts me to you.

Doubt. Delayed doubt.

Andrew arrived, his cupped hands overflowing with pastries and Arabic sweets. Sara was perplexed. Where *was* Father getting all this money from? And if he has so much, why was he wasting it on *her*? Wasn't she usually the forgotten child?

'Don't worry, there is enough here for us to take back to Mimmy and Daud,' he said, 'You want to ride this camel?' He observed her acute attachment towards the child camel, which had now finished feeding.

She nodded. *Why do you bribe me as if you are guilty?*

'Come on, we'll finish quickly. A small round of Aden port and we'll be back before they wake up.'

Immersed in between reeds of reluctance, Sara knew that she didn't want to go, everything was just becoming unrealistic. Too much stardust for one night. Helena's stern warnings rattled inside her head: 'Don't go out with Father alone, Sara. Don't go out with Andrew.' Maternal instinct- why had she gone against it? She looked over her shoulder to see what Andrew was doing- he had already paid one of the camel drivers.

She panicked. What shall I do? What is he going to do to me? I can't run away- in between the flocks of men. I'll easily be caught. She touched her numbing forehead in exasperation. Trying to calm her nerves down, she firmly repeated to herself that nothing was going to happen to her. Andrew for once, was not drunk, and he was in a clear state of mind to take her back home. Home to Mother, Mimmy and Daud.

Mimmy caught sight of Sara's hair being tamed by the wind. She was tired of walking between funny figures of strange men. She wanted to cuddle into Mother's familiar, floppy, bosom. Hurrying on, she tried to catch sight of Sara. But she couldn't. All she could see were men dressed in white; some with yellow stains under their arms, some without. She was not scared - as a child of her age normally would be. Often Andrew brought her to shops and little outings.

A cart, which strongly let out a scent of mocha coffee beans, caught her attention. It was a small cart, with a thick brown quilt of coffee beans spread out in the back. Soft, brown, velvety coffee beans. The smell reminded her of Father, and she went and waited for him near it. Father liked this smell, so he must be coming near it. But her legs were tired and wobbly, and she was restless, so she went inside and threw the beans all over herself. Father would find her. She knew he would.

Despite the emerging clearness of the air, it was not a pleasant ride. Andrew was riding beside her, on a much stronger and larger camel, yet she didn't feel *safe*. Something was in that mind of his. She rocked between the humps of the child camel. She clutched the hump in front of her for comfort. It was soft, sensitive. Fragile. Feeble. 'Feeble as me,' she sighed.

The sky cracked open to a collage of vivid colours as dawn approached. Purples, pinks, oranges and reds merged and contrasted with one another, giving a stark silhouette to the ebony ships and boats in the distance. Other carts laden with goods were going in the same direction, towards Aden port for trade. They formed a maze of lanes leading to the ship in their large quantities. The tradesmen walked either silently beside their mules or if they had camels, they rode on them with a serious air about them. In both cases, they would ritually stop every so often, and offer their animals a drink and give a reassuring pat on their backs. It was undeniable that Sara was magnetised by the midnight adventure, but simultaneously she missed her mother. She was averted at the same time. Repulsed by Andrew, who was busy calculating something on his fingers. She felt guilty, since he did so much for her, but for the first time she felt that there was some wisdom in Mother's words. She felt she was colliding with Mother Nature's advice, almost surrendering to a moral battle. She was uncomfortable. Then there was Daud's cold, bitter treatment towards Father. There had to be a reason. She just wished she knew what it was.

The sea threw down its cloak of waves on the rocky shore, as if in defence to their sharp, irregular edges. The largest black ship wobbled on its hull like a gigantic floating apple. A smokey eyed steersman paused to sip cooled tea, glancing guardedly over the rim of the wooden cup as he hoped for a customer.

'Well, here we are! Come off Sara!' Andrew shouted, dragging her shin off the camel.

'Here, are we going to stay *here*? But we were meant to be home before dawn. Let's turn back.' She pulled her leg back from him. 'We'll be late back home,' she managed to whisper. His grasp didn't loosen. Instead, he wrenched her off fiercely. A small muscle tightened and snapped in her legs. Her box tumbled into the sand. 'What are you doing?' she demanded tearfully, trying to free herself from his suffocating grip.

'Sending you to have a better life.' he muttered spitefully. He hauled her with an animal-like strength through the coarse sand granules. Her splashing legs blew up a miniature dust storm around them. She managed to pick up her box with her free hand and tuck it under her dress.

'HELP! Help!!!!'

Then, came something that burnt Sara's courage to free herself altogether. He pulled her hair back, tight and spoke harshly into her ear. 'Don't you dare make a noise hear me? Don't you dare. You owe me all of this, all these years I have fed you and kept you under *my* roof. You would have made me more money if you were a prostitute!'

The words felt like swallowing white, searing, scorching live coals. Her skin split, unable to react. Her world, her dreams, her happiness crushed before her. Crush, crash, thump. Everything was an illusion. *What* was he suggesting? That he never loved her? She *was* the forgotten child? Once a forgotten child, always forgotten. That's what she forgot. In shock, the tears froze inside her heart and she felt each tiny bead pierce her chest, one by one. In her grief, she did not notice the trail of camel carts approaching the deck. Inside were huddles of women, some draped in black, others in their own clothing, being offloaded like cargo and being sent into the massive black ship. Sara was thrust in between them too, toppling into crumbs like a child's mud ball.

The ship was surrounded with canoes ranging all sizes. The prow of the ship rose elegant and slender, breaking the sky into two. Behind the ship was a new world, in front was another fading world. A brightly coloured mosaic of sea birds filled the sky, the hard stone tiles being replaced with soft delicate feathers. It was a smooth switch.

'I'd like to sell this one as a maid,' Andrew shouted to the man in charge of operations.

'Any relation to you?'

'None.' He took a deep breath. 'None whatsoever,' he confirmed, this time with authority. He slammed his fist on the railing, demanding a quick process.

Hearing what he had said, Sara stared at the floor so that he would not see her tears. The tears pulled her face into the ground with their weight. *What is my own father doing? Selling me? He just gave me life to serve as cheap labour for him?* She looked up at him one last time, praying that this was not happening. To her horror, he had accepted silver coins, which he jingled between his fingers mercilessly.

'Father!' she cried, and then plucking up her courage, 'ANDREW you can't leave me here!' Water streamed out of her eyes in duplex hoses, thrashing down her face with the force of an erupting tropical volcano. As he walked out of her heart, a silent, violent cascade of emotion followed with the downward force of a waterfall. And like reality, the impact began and ended at the foot of it.

Her protesting squeals were ignored.

Slap.

The assault came from a large, gruesome looking woman.

'It's no use child. Once you are sold, you are sold. The deal is sealed.'

'But I'm certain he's drugged. He is not thinking with his mind. I am his daughter. He's tipsy! Tipsy! You must believe me. I'm certain….'

'Nothing in life is certain. The only thing that you can be absolutely sure of is death. Death will come to everything and everyone.' She said this with a sternness, as if she had repeated it a million times, such that even she didn't want to except the fact anymore.

'But I'm his daughter!' she hiccupped, watching him abandon her.

'If you were, he would never have done this to you. Now go inside,' the irritated woman reasoned, pushing her roughly into the ship. 'He has blotted you out of his life in a single swipe. Teach yourself to do the same. Young men can't be trusted'

Sara fell clumsily against the wall, knowing that she had no choice but to obey, and to take her position between the hundreds of ladies in the swelling ship. Compact baby chicks in a basket. *I am an orphan despite having parents!* Letting her body slip down onto the floor, she stared at the blurred image of the box in her lap.

Life: raft in the sea.

Her life: whirlpools and thunder. Without the raft.

Mimmy was soon discovered by a coffee trader, sleeping peacefully in between the caressing coat of coffee.

'What are you doing?' he demanded, amazed to find a little girl in his cart. 'Where did you come from? Shoo! Go away!'

'No!'

'No?'

'No!'

Puzzled at what he should do, he attempted to track down the whereabouts of her parents, but 'No!' was the only answer he got. Contemplating that this was the most information he could expect from the stubborn girl, he walked around and saw if anyone claimed to have lost a child. For a while, he hunted patiently for her parents, but then he realised he had to get back to the suq to get the second load of coffee. He didn't know what to do. The most he could do was leave her here. If he took her with him, her parents might come back and would get worried. He saw the plump manager of the large black ship, chatting away. 'Ah he must know something, he looks responsible.'

'Excuse me sir. This child was found- I can not find her parents. If you could be so kind to stay with her and wait for her parents to arrive, Allah will be pleased with you.'

'Where did you find her?'

'Sleeping in my cart.'

The manager examined Mimmy who had large brown eyes and her yellow little frock on. 'Yes, alright then,' he agreed, not paying much attention since he had many other dealings to oversee.

Mimmy stood beside the manager, holding his hand impatiently, looking out for Andrew. She tried to wriggle out of his grasp, but he was too strong. No one came for her, and the full crown of the sun was soon expected.

He decided to put her on the ship where maybe one of the women would want to adopt her. He picked her up.

'Father! Father! Father!' she screamed as loudly as she could.

The manager stopped, and put her down, waiting for someone to appear. 'Do it again,' he urged.

So she did.

But no one came for her.

The port eventually was sucked barren, and silence swooped the shore. The commotion faded into small, lingering dots.

'I can't keep the ship waiting any longer,' said the manager 'You will have to come with me onto the ship,' he added softly.

'No! Father and Sara are here.' She dropped to the floor. 'Father and Sara' she repeated. Finally, her apparent buoyancy was diluted with silent sobs.

'They are not here, my dear. Come, you must be hungry, I'll

give you some milk,' he said, touched by the innocence of the girl as he walked into the ship.

'We're ready to leave for Jeddah,' he commanded one of his men.

'Right,' the sailor replied. He hurried off to repeat the order to the Captain.

ᒼ ᒼ ᒼ ᒼ ᒼ ᒼ ᒼ ᒼ ᒼ ᒼ
◇◇◇◇◇◇◇◇◇◇◇◇◇◇◇◇◇◇◇◇

Many things combined to splurge out the beams of deep golden hope emitting from his crinkly face. Andrew paddled in the sand, it swaddled his hard ankles with its soft fine granules. His eyes were set on the distance before him – the path that would give him freedom, freedom from sweat! The air was progressively becoming warmer, and when the rosy red sun bobbed out from behind the thick creamy shore the extra perspiration did not bother him. Sweat trickled, in almost parallel lines on his face, webbing it with glistening moisture. His skin turned a buttery yellow, like a freshly baked batch of bread.

He wondered what he could do with the money first. He could spend it carefully. He could treat himself once in a while, but then the rest should sustain him for quite a time. He stopped in his tracks. He had to repay Cynthia for the gold bangle he took off her. He'd get her a nice present to make up for it. She'd be amazed at the sight of all the money too! He felt a tingling sensation between his thighs at the thought of his lover's reaction.

A rattling cart pulled by a lame, feeble looking donkey caught up with him. Andrew stared at it, finding relief that he would *not* have to be working in old age. Crippling beggars took a lot of strength and he wisely anticipated that he could not rely on this trade forever. His dear Mimmy would take care of him. His dear darling Mimmy. At the thought of his little daughter he smiled. He'd get her married to a rich young man and live in peace. Helena didn't have many days left and Daud, Daud was his embarrassment. His only son was his acute weakness. He was meant to be his strength – but he crippled him, like one of his own mutated products. Deep down inside Andrew knew that he himself was to blame for his son's reluctance towards him. His chest was heavy, somewhat loaded with pain, grief and loss at the thought that Daud would desert him after Helena died. But still, he consoled himself with visions of security: At least he'd have Mimmy.

'Father!' 'Father!'

He could hear her voice. It was almost real. He could hear it faintly, but it sounded as if Mimmy was wailing. It was coming from a distance. Mimmy was around somewhere.

'Father!'

He turned around to look at the ship, which was sailing away. It was coming from the ship. The ship? But how would Mimmy have got there. Wasn't she sleeping safely at home?

'Father NOOooooooo!' At the sound of this shrill shriek he was convinced that Mimmy was aboard the ship. He didn't know *how,* but she was on the ship for sure. Present somehow. He panicked. He speeded towards the ship, alarmed. His feet swamped into the sand with each forceful stride. Tears of regret burst from his eye ducts onto his face, intermingling with the droplets of rogueness that were just swiped across his face a moment ago.

'Mimmy! Mimmy wait!'

The cart drivers, their donkeys, mules and even camels were puzzled at the man who was running as if his life was ripping apart. Heart in one direction, mind in the other. Andrew's legs gave way. He felt a muscle tightening in his left leg and he fell with tremendous force into the ground. Snap. Gravity tugged him down so hard that the muddy sand went spraying – almost flying from underneath to cover him like fleeing ants somersaulting in the air. He tried to get up with all his might but his efforts were of no use. The sand scoured face watched the ship sail away into the bright white distance.

They were in a chicken coup. At least that's exactly what it felt like. Sara hatched, a pink, raw newborn out of the shell she longed to get back into. She skimmed through the hundreds of faces around her. It was clear that she was the youngest girl present in the ship. Some faces were shattered, some pale with torture and others, though very few, appeared relieved. The floor she was sitting on was damp and smelly from all the human sweat scooped into the area. She turned away, disgusted. The woman-cargo was fully loaded, each sold for some odd reason. Every so often a guard would come to monitor the farm of ladies that surrounded his feet like a field of human grass.

She was parcelled like an object sent away in the post. The girth of love shrunk around her, the band choking her with each violent compression. Fury tore strips of her apart. Sara was scared. Deep down inside she knew nothing of what was going to happen to her. She was an orphan now, a member of the unwanted nobody group, like the ones she pitied in the market who wore foul smelling rags and waved their bowls in passer-byer's faces. Her bloodshot eyes were stinging as if she had put her head above a smoky fire. Splinters pinched and calloused her eyeballs. Stabbing pain. She prayed that somehow she could get back home, but she knew she never would. *Why* had she listened to Father? Why? The spears in his last few words were tearing her to pieces:

'Any relation to you?'

'None whatsoever.'

'I am his daughter!'

'Any relation to you?'

'None whatsoever.'

'I am his daughter!'

'You don't have a drop of my blood. Now get inside!'

Well if she wasn't Andrew's daughter whose daughter was she? And why did Father live with them then? Maybe Mother was forced to live with him. Maybe that's why she was so cold towards him. Sara forced herself to reason in order to take control of her own thoughts and not vice versa. What about Daud and Mimmy? Would she ever see them again? She felt as if a vacuum was sucking the life out of her. She was shrivelled up for good.

'Father! Father, No!'

Sara heard the faint wail from the ceiling.

'Father…Sara! Father!' the voice repeated.

Sara could not believe her ears – she wanted to make sure that she was not hallucinating.

'Now, now child, are you hungry?' asked a man's deep voice – in such a way that it was obvious that talking to children was not something he was familiar with.

Had Father sold Mimmy *too*? He was a mongrel. A true mongrel. Immediately, Sara shot to her feet. 'That's my sis…. daughter, my daughter'

All eyes were focused on her.

'Give me my daughter!'

'Sit down' the guard motioned her, 'and be quiet.' He thought Sara was insane to be making out that the little girl was her daughter. Why, this young girl was too young herself.

'I promise you Sir, I look young, but that girl *is* related to me. You can compare the similarities on our faces. We have the same eyes, nose and face. Just please, give me my daughter!' she pleaded. In a way she was not lying, Sara *was* Mimmy's mother since she was the daily baby-sitter. If they were mother and daughter no one could separate them. The scraggly women sitting at her feet, cushioning her like a carpet, were temporarily jolted out of their sob stories and watched the live entertainment before them. Sara felt the long, warm rays penetrating from their eyes into her.

'Mimmy, Mimmy!' She shouted as loudly as her throat allowed her.

'Sara? Sara!' Mimmy recognised her sister's voice.

The guard, after all this commotion, went to call the manager and the child. Sara felt pleased and hoped to God it was Mimmy. It was safer that she would be with her rather than be exposed to Father's disloyal wrath. He would scavenge her too. She stood silently waiting for him to return Mimmy to her.

The guard appeared with Mimmy and the manager. 'You are telling me she is her *mother*?' asked the manager in a mocking tone.

'Yes sir, see how their faces look alike.'

The manager put Mimmy on the floor and compared both their faces. Yes, it was no doubt that they were related – but such a young mother? He tried to convince himself. It was impossible. What was the world coming to? He had heard that Egyptian women aged very slowly, since they had less frequent child births.

She must be one of them.

Sara hoped that Mimmy, for once, would not let out a word. Mimmy, talkative and stubborn as she was, did not, to her relief.

'Very well, go to your mother,' the manager said, smiling at Mimmy.

Mimmy ran in between the pebbles of ladies to reach Sara. Sara picked her up and hugged her, squeezing her so emotionally that some of the ladies' sullen faces broke into a smile.

A young messenger presented himself to the manager. 'Sir, Sheikh Khalil has ordered to halt the ship. He has sent a carriage for a handful of women to work at his palace.'

Silently the manager nodded and turned away.

Sara noticed none of this. She put Mimmy in her lap and kissed her. 'Did Father sell you too?' she asked quietly.

'No, I followed you. You and Father. Father is on the boat too.' She ran her small fingers through Sara's hair.

'You followed us?' Sara could hardly believe her ears at first, but realised that since Mimmy was not with them on the journey that's the only way she could have come onto the ship. 'No Mimmy, Father has left us. He is not on the ship.'

'Left us?'

'Yes, he has deserted us.'

'He'll come for us in the morning,' Mimmy yawned and nuzzled into Sara's body for padding.

'Maybe he will,' Sara replied, more than aware that he wouldn't. Besides, by then they'd be in a different country altogether. Was it Jeddah that they were going? Hell, she didn't care.

A red haired woman caught her attention, since her head was partly uncovered. She stood out like blood on a white towel. Ghostly pale, her intense ruffle of hair emitted a steady heat without flames. The bright shadow of her head flushed a lively essence into her face as she tilted sideways to straighten her back. Unusually for a red haired person, her face was not spotted with freckles. Sara always hated that. Freckles were like albino flies swimming in milk. Whilst she continued glummering over destiny, the red haired woman drew closer, barging through the swamp of women.

'I say, aren't you Helena's daughter?' asked the lady hoarsely, three feet away from where Sara and Mimmy were sitting.

Not knowing what to say, Sara nodded.

'So you must be Sara. I worked with her for years in the same outlet. But then after a few years she become ill and had to leave. I also lost my youthfulness and had to become a waitress.'

'What is your name?' asked Sara, quite amused that someone actually knew her without her even meeting them. She felt privileged to be related to a celebrity.

'Lisa,' she whispered, very very quietly so that Sara had to bend over to listen.

'That's a nice name.'

'You were a glamorous star too?'

'For a little while—'

'You…you are Helena's daughter?' said an Arab lady. 'If I could get my hands on that bitch. She ruined my marriage, look at where I am now. She ruined my brother's marriage. What do you expect from a Jew!'

'A *Jew*!' An immediate reaction of astonishment that ran through the huddles in waves.

Sara stared at Lisa for help, totally confused.

Lisa motioned her not to worry. 'They can't do anything – they're in the same position as us. Puppets to be bought and sold. Are you in the same business?'

'Oh no.' Sara was startled by how easily this woman was

ignoring the stir between the women. 'I sew dolls and Father goes and sells them!'

'That's good,' said Lisa smiling at Sara. 'Helena never wanted her daughters to become a victim of poverty and tiredness like herself.'

'Poverty and tiredness?' asked Sara. Her mother's luxurious belongings spoke otherwise.

'Poverty and tiredness.' Lisa confirmed. 'I say tiredness instead of helplessness because I offered her a way out. She could have spent her life with me, we could have brought you lot up together. But she was scared. Terrified of the idea of bringing up children without a father. I used to say, how could she confirm that you three were Andrew's anyway? Is she still with that mongrel Andrew?'

'Yes. He lives with us.' The incorrect tense collided in her chest.

'She didn't leave him in the end?'

'No.'

'I guess he's the one who sold you two then.'

'Yes.'

'He's disgusting. He used to beat your mother and take all of her earnings. He forced her into a life that no woman ever wants to be part of.'

'But...she had wonderful clothes. She was a singer....'

Sara objected, wondering what on earth Father forced Mother to do. 'She was a singer alright. She wore fancy clothes. Fancy clothes that Andrew gave her to tantalise *other* men. To seduce them into her love.'

Sara gulped, tears welling in her eyes. Her mother was a... was a...the word was not even coming to her head. All these years she had thought her mother was respectable. Both her parents were sickening. Both!

I hate you both. What is the use of us respecting you if you behave like this?

Lisa put her arms around Sara. 'She never wanted to do it. None of us did. Our husbands or uncles or someone else threatened us. No woman ever wants to be a toy, a decoration piece for the sore eyes of love-hungry men. Ever. If she does, then there is something Satanic about her.'

'But I was positive, that my mother was respectable.' Tears trickled down her face at the unmasking of reality before her. 'We were religious. We are God fearing people...' She sobbed. *Is this all we're worth? Motherhood or whoredom? Extreme opposites! Is that it?*

'You may fear God, but some people never fear God. They are evil. Evil like Andrew.'

'I'm certain that...,' Sara tried to gather her splattered feelings together.

'Certain? Certain my dear, nothing's certain in life. Nothing. The only thing that is ever certain in life that will happen to you is Death. That is it. Death and only death.'

This was the second time that this was mentioned to her like an omen of some sort and so Sara figured that it must be true. But before Sara could ponder on the magnitude of Lisa's words, two guards entered. One was tall, the other was short. In fact they were both so opposite that it seemed as if they had deliberately paired up to show everyone how contrasting they were.

'Sheikh Khalil has ordered for a handful of maidens to be sent to the palace to work. I will choose eight women to be employed in his residence.' He pointed his stick at ladies that looked young and youthful.

'Kaleem,' echoed the manager's voice from behind. 'I've

decided that we should send the mother and daughter that were reunited today.'

'*Them*? But they are far too young.'

'They look young. But it will be best for them,' said the manager smiling at the sight of sleeping Mimmy between Sara's arms.

'But Sheikh Khalil will not approve.' The guard was unexpectedly nervous.

'He will. Come on both of you. Up. You are going to be maids in the Sheikh's residence.'

Sara stood up shakily. Mimmy was sleeping in her arms. She had no choice, at least they would stay in Yemen now, maybe, just maybe she'll meet Daud again. She wasn't sure if she wanted to meet Mother. Well, not yet anyway. Not until her idol had been rebuilt piece by piece.

'Follow me.'

The ship came to a halt. It stopped back at the shore to let the Sheikh's orders be carried out. It's dark wooden hull beckoned dangerously in the water that was sloshing its sides. Seven women together with Sara and Mimmy were off loaded from the ship. To Sara's relief, the Arab women who had finger-pointed at Helena were not part of the selection. As she followed the dark, damp, blue lit alleyways in the ship she knew she had to do two things to ensure her and Mimmy's safety.

Just now she had been exposed to a possible threat, the fact that she was a Jew. She didn't know why it mattered, it never was an issue in the neighbourhood or Rawda Square – but it could be in big, foreign places. She must pretend to be a Muslim. Adopt a Muslim name. Arabs called their females Miriam so that didn't matter, but she was not sure about 'Sara.' She had never heard it before. Secondly, Mimmy must remain as her daughter. She knew it was very hard to believe, but for the time being that was just the way it would have to be. There was no other choice.

Fooled once, fooled twice.

Chapter 8

Late that evening…

In the corner of Rawda square, Andrew sank into the arm-rests in the darkest part of the brewery. The dim candlelight flickered at him as if it wanted to burn brighter but couldn't in the suffocating air. *How* did Mimmy get on the ship? How did Mimmy get on the ship? The questions pinched him repetitively, like a needling mosquito bite. Maybe God punished him for using Sara. A penalty: punishment for the first time he had received, not the first time had earned it.

'Last orders! Last orders!' screamed the waiter. 'Last orders,' he yelled into Andrew's corner.

Andrew spent the entire day gurgling down wine and liquor (the strongest, bitterest kind) to wash away the stains on his conscience. Poor Mimmy. He remembered when she was born how she snuggled up cosily into the incurvation of his chest and the way she had held his finger with her miniature clammy pink ones and soaked them in drool from her tiny red mouth. She was a baby rabbit, tiny and ever so delicate. And she was *his*, his *own* daughter. After her birth, he even stopped Helena from working. Yes, he had a special fondness for Mimmy – one which he never found in his son.

He had drunk so much alcohol that he was gloating in guilt. He wallowed in sweaty alcohol stained clothes. He was literally a smelly burp bubble. The once impressive appearance was peeled off. The bumpy forehead's surface, now noticeably darkened, gleamed with sin, sweat and sorrow. For the first time, Andrew Bengen sat with his head lowered. Not just slightly bent, but fully inclined at a perfect right angle.

'Oh God forgive me! What was I thinking? I have always taken from which did not belong to me. Now You have taken something from me, because I returned one of your blessings! Please, show me mercy. My heart is splitting too fast for me to glue back together!' he said to God. 'I can't be blamed! I can't. How did Mimmy get on the ship? What games do you play my Lord, what games?' Anger swirled in his belly venomously. 'I won't surrender. I'll fight the battle like a man!' Alcohol sloshed down his throat with the velocity of a turbulent river. He slammed his fist on the wall, trying to break the nib of the exasperation which pinched him.

'Sir, you must leave now,' said the noisy waiter. To his dismay, Andrew was lying unconscious against the muddy straw wall. He hurried to tell his supervisor to be given instructions on what to do next. The brewery would be shut down if there was a scandal.

Two other waiters and the supervisor hurled him up and tried to shape him back into the seat. He was in putty consistency. They padded his face with a towel soaked in cool, icy water.

'He's been here since the morning, very much disturbed about something,' reported the young waiter, Zebed.

'Maybe his wife betrayed him,' said the elder of the waiters.

'No need to talk nonsense. Only speak what you must,' said the supervisor firmly, wondering how many times he had told his employees that.

'Now let's pick him up and put him outside, we can't keep him here. We'll receive punishment from the Muttawas[1] if he finds we overdosed him. Weren't any of you watching?'

Both dropped their heads.

'Miserable swines.' He was agitated that his brewery was threatened with closure if the Muttawas found out that they had a drugged customer.

'He offered us silver,' whispered Zebed.

'Silver?' said the manager. 'And you all kept pouring him with alcohol? Shame on you. Now get up and stay with him until he gains consciousness. You must be held responsible for your neglect. Now don't you leave until he regains his senses.'

The two waiters stood beside Andrew until he woke back to life but after a while, even they flopped down beside him, tired from a hard days work.

'It's your fault Isaac. I told you not to accept the silver no matter how much it enticed you,' said Zebed.

'Fool, don't you see it was worth it. What is one day's staying awake compared to all the silver he gave us? We don't make that much in a month.'

'But we'll lose our jobs.'

'No we won't. Simon is too wary that we could go and tell a Muttawa and his business will be shut down. Now, we can blackmail him.'

'Blackmail him?'

'Yes, blackmail him,'

'That's wrong. I'm leaving,' said Zebed. 'Simon gave me a job, clothes, everything I needed without asking any questions about where I came from. In Spain, we never did things like this. You are a backstabbing rat.' He stood stiff, clenching his fists and ready to leave. He looked pathetic, trying to be tough, like a stork trying to show off its bulk.

Isaac already laid out a trap for him. Sniggering, he pushed the window open towards the door so that his accomplice could not escape. As planned, he tripped. He fell flat on his face.

'Leave me alone Isaac. Leave me alone. I don't want to be a part of it,' the young boy stammered, tears burst out onto his face, as much as he tried to stop them.

Dragging him back in, his clothes ripping against the pink granite flooring, Isaac forced him into the wall. 'My boy, you already are a part of this. Now listen to what I have to say.' The saliva shot at Zebed's face in liquid pellets.

Andrew unfurled his drunken eyes. He felt mutilated and lifeless. The tufts of Ilb plant roots in the roof above gaped at him. The branches clapped together. The leaves sang. Nothing was real. His head ached, he couldn't feel his soul. He yelled, interrupting the two waiters who released one another from their grip.

'I see you have come to your senses, old man,' said Isaac. He completely forgot his quarrel with Zebed.

'Yes.' Andrew stood up in a stumble, with the help of Zebed. 'I must get home.' He swayed in his stance.

Isaac obstructed his leave, and insisted that he assess if Andrew was well enough to go home by himself. He grabbed him savagely by the shoulders and shook him.

'I'm fine,' he said. He walked out resembling a curious figure who was stiff with sin and swaying with sacrifice consecutively. Soaked in his alcoholic oblivion, Andrew ploughed his journey home. His head was numb and nauseated. All he wanted to do was to lie down, next to Mimmy and tell her a story, kind of like the ones Cynthia used to tell him when he was a boy.

Under the thick velvet of the night, he approached their hut, feeling something loop heavily around his right leg. Old Winona caught him by the foot.

'I know what you have done,' she said scowling so horrifyingly that he kicked her aside and burst into the hut in fright. She didn't react; she was immune to any form of worldly pain.

His face clouded into a fog as the unblinking eerie masks welcomed him.

'Where are my children? Where are my children!' Helena leapt upon him like a predator. 'What have you done?' She shook him, unable to contain the scorching heat firing up inside her. She was a mother and she was mad. Everyone knows that a combination of these two features are the most feared in a human. The splinters didn't affect Andrew. Words burned on her tongue in silent agony.

'What have you *done?*' Daud sneered, pushing Andrew fiercely into the floor. At this assault, a few of the remaining silver coins clinked to the dust-smothered floor.

To Andrew, they were more like clangs.

Daud didn't wait. He knew that his father had sold his sisters at the sight of the silver. He clasped his fingers around Andrew's thick neck. The natural friction between them multiplied to an unbearable climax.

'You swine! You sold my sisters!'

Andrew, trying to escape from his son's grip, pushed his feet against the wall, where Helena stood frozen solid like a monument, crying. His legs fiercely lunged at her feeble stick ones.

She fell.

Daud, on seeing this, punched Andrew. He needed to pulverise this parasite once and for all. Andrew managed to escape his son's attacks and stumbled into Helena.

She was now sitting in a helpless pile on the floor. As he darted towards her, rage ravaged her mind. Frantically she pulled and tugged his hair as if her life depended on it. She struck him for all the silver he bartered her daughters for. Andrew, being attacked from both sides charged at Helena, who fell forcefully into the wall. Her eyes looked upwards to the ceiling and she fell, revealing a straight, gory blood stain as her head slid to the floor. Blood bathed around her in a puddle.

The candle light meandered on the wall. Doom stepped in to the picture.

'You killed my Mother too!' Daud could not believe his eyes. This was NOT happening. He ran to her, but there was no response. He tried to flip her back to life.

Andrew, still trying to get back to his senses, looked at them, unable to understand what he had done.

Daud didn't waste any time. He got hold of the largest Jambilya knife they owned and propelled it directly into his father. Over and over and over.

The honey bottle fell out of his pocket and cracked with the magnitude of action.

The stabs were deep, piercing, penetrating. One after the other landed like a well rehearsed devil dance of exorcism. Daud slotted the knife and wrenched the hook into the man's body that lay before him like a watermelon asking to be sliced.

Gash after gash pleaded justice. After about thirty slashes Daud decided he had had enough.

They both had had enough.

[1] Religious police

Burzukh

With black scaly skin, hair erect as fluorescent bolts and smoke emitting from his crusty nose and mouth in pointy cones, his face hovered above her. The crevice was swarthy and sullen as it was, yet his single eye protruded so far ahead of his nose that she thought the filmy surface of the eyeball was touching her.

His toxic stench suffocated her.

The Watchful Eye humiliated her.

Black scaly skin made her quiver out of her own.

Thundering upon her with his ear-piercing scream he gave her her tiding. It could be one of two things:

'Rejoice, O'enemy of God, at the prospect of Hell!'

'Rejoice O'friend of God, at the prospect of Heaven!'

Whatever her justified fate was, Arwa had to stay patiently in the waiting room, Burzukh, until everyone who was ever born was visited by the Angel of Death.

She sat on her seat nervously, the surrounding seats not yet occupied. The intermediate realm was struck with silence. Souls looked worried, others perspired, and many battered themselves on the misty grey floor. Everyone was preoccupied. She considered her personal scales, about the Grand Inquisition that would proclaim all Great and Small in front of everyone.

Yearning for an intimate conversation, she felt a gentle tap on her shoulder. She sensed the taps pass through her form. She almost leapt out of her skin, unaccustomed to soul interaction. It was a middle aged man who looked familiar, yet she could not recognise who it was.

Sara my dear, I am your father,' he announced.

She felt the plug of sanity being eased out of her. Glug. Glug. Glug. My father? This was not her father. Her father was Andrew. 'I am sorry sir, you are mistaken, I already have a father,' she replied.

He sat down beside her. 'No Sara, I am your *real* father. Andrew was a man whom Helena married again after our divorce.' His eyes remained fixated at the pink smoke swirling around his ankles. 'I want to apologise. You were my only child. I left you both, because I did not want to be a burden on you.'

How could this man be my father, how? And why did Mother never tell me?

The transparent informal attitude was reflected in the atmosphere. The irony was that they all were present to attend a formality. She stared at him in disbelief. She had had a faceless father all along and Mother never told her? Her mind worked three times as fast as it did on Earth. Perhaps she should forgive Andrew – he adopted her and cared for her, despite Sara not being his own. Yes, she would forgive him. If she did not, God would not forgive her either.

The white sleeves of his thin robe flapped around him with excessive flexibility. They rolled in the shape of the wind, resembling enlarged floating socks. A sleeve blew into the air and rested on her lap. Before she could react, he cut her off.

'I had no arms. They were cut off because I stole a silver candle stick holder from one of my clients to support you both. I don't know what came over me. I was a respectable carpenter. Helena and I eloped from Turkey to Yemen since your grandfather did not approve of our alliance.' He quietly sobbed. 'For a few weeks Helena managed, with you being so young, but I was defected, impaired for life. There was no work I could do. I couldn't even hold my own child.' Tears appeared at the base of his eyelids in an icy crust, but were immediately evaporated by a coloured breeze. 'So I left. I was more a burden then help. Without me Helena could re-marry and secure a future for you. She was beautiful, a capable and honourable young woman.' Once more the tears squeezed out but curiously were eaten up in a matter of moments by the same tinted swirls.

'But why did he not approve?'

'Because I was a Turkish Muslim. And she was a Spanish Jew. Your grandfather forgot that it was my brothers who welcomed him in Ottoman, he forgot that it was my brothers who extended a shelter of security around him. He forgot that it was us who let their race survive from the Christians and not let it be extinct. All he could see was that I was a Muslim. That is one thing he would not let himself forget. Helena wanted to remain a Jew and I respected her for it. But all this was ignored. All that was visible was my cultural identity. Allah granted me the worst punishment of all: watching the consequences of my actions. Day after day I witnessed Helena sell herself to survive.' He paused suddenly, shifting in tone, as if realising something, recalling something obscure about the girl that stood before him. 'Forgive me, my daughter. I tried so hard to give you what I did not have that I forgot to give you what I did have.'

Arwa raised her eyes to meet his.

It was apparent that he was aware of all her actions since he had slipped into the waiting room. He knew exactly what she had endured. She could not put anything out of sight. She had nothing to hide.

Although he was still unfamiliar to her, she felt a growing ease tugging her towards him. 'And what did you have which I didn't?' she asked. She smiled in response to the light he had shed on matters.

'Anyone worthy of being called your own,' he replied. He rolled his eyes heavenward.

Chapter 9

Daud ran: hot, sticky sweat spurting on his body like a fountain. He sped between the dark smelly alleyways in their hilly plain. He whirred past the prostitute house where Andrew spent his days working. He ran past Winona, who slept curled up in a dusty space between two walls, sheltered by the mass of shaggy hair that was vegetating on her head.

Scared, flustered and tired, he halted when he was a few miles away from home at the empty market place, the suq. He shot weary glances to his left and right. Front and back. Right and left. No one was around. He had to get away from the smell, the horrible raw vapour of Andrew's leaking blood that was galloping after him, like a tail. He sank to the floor, lifeless.

Mother was dead. Father killed her.

Father was dead. Daud killed him.

What he had done was not wrong. It just was not. Anyone could see that. Father –Andrew – had sold his sisters, sold them! Sold his own daughters for a few silver coins. Shiny, glinting evil coins. What kind of a man was he? What kind of a father was he? A bastard. That's what Andrew was. And he was the bastard's son. Bastards were always like that: they can't trust anyone so they couldn't be trusted themselves either.

Shutting his rashy pink eyelids, he recalled how Sara and Mimmy used to play with him. How Mother used to fondle his hair, and tell him off mockingly. How, how, how?

The first tear squirted out of the corner of his right eye. It acted as a signal to the hot springs that followed. His entire family was hurled up and shot around randomly. Some parts were gone. Some parts were decaying. Some parts were lost. And he had to watch it all. The sad part was that he could not take part in the game. He was a pawn – but the kind of pawns which are taken off the board because they were out, watching from a distance.

A cool, calming breeze blew on his face. He was *not* guilty. He just was not guilty. He wasn't scared of being caught. There was no point in living himself anymore. Everything he had ever done was for others. But there were no others now. Except for Deborah. But would she even accept him? He wasn't sure.

The breeze blew again, rolling a liquor vessel slowly in his direction. It stopped right in front of him. Daud picked it up, and stared at it with such veracity that it was a wonder that the flame blasted bottle did not shatter to pieces in his hands. 'You are the reason why Andrew did all this. *You.* You put him out of his mind, you sick addiction,' he said. Venom fizzed between his gritted teeth. He thrust the vessel down on the paving stone next to him.

The pieces went flying everywhere; some flew so far that they could not even be seen. That's what liquor did to his family. Nerves tingling, and rumbling hot with turbulent emotions, he stood up. He would find out what it is about liquor, what Satanic power it possessed, that steers a man into behaving so irrationally. He made his way to the cursed area of the village. He knew he would get his answer there.

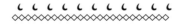

Slowly, Helena opened her eyes. She could not focus. She drew up her frail hand in front of her face in an attempt to see something in the reduced candle light. She tried to gather herself together mentally. She was pushed, hard and firmly against the wall; she had felt the air being squeezed out of her flimsy chest.

She grasped the pole of her bed stand and managed to stand up, on the wetness. Where was everyone? She turned around and saw Andrew, lying helplessly like a lamb chop on the floor, a pool of blood filling the area around him. She looked at her feet. She was standing in a raw puddle of blood. It took a few moments for her numb head to deduce what had happened, or at least what she thought had happened. Andrew was dead. Daud must have killed him. Her daughters were in foreign lands. Her son, scared that both his parents were dead, had ran away.

Helena never wanted any of this. She tried her best to protect her children from harm, from the muck of poverty that everyone was forced into. But all that tension and effort erupted right before her eyes. It was like she was balancing on the edge of a volcano's crater, trying to plug the dip aimlessly with everything she could. It blasted everything away, all together, in one puff. Her daughters were destined to be prostitutes now. Her son was a murderer and her dead husband was to blame for all this. Her blood was up. Poison quaked in her veins, splattering through pores on her skin.

Tears didn't come rolling out this time. No, she was not going to let them. She fought them back into the ducts, lifting them up with courage. Infuriated, she picked up the knife that lay at her feet and clenched it hard between her hands. She stomped over to Andrew, breathing heavily, grunting like a wolf searching for its prey, printing the floor with vulgar footprints. She fell on her knees next to him. The blood drenched her white dress, climbing upwards from the hem right up to her hips in wonky lines.

She pounced on him. She stabbed him fiercely as many times as she could, like a savage, tribal man cutting wood for dinner. Shlink! Shlink! Shlink! The blade of the knife sniggered as it poked and withdrew randomly from Andrew's body. She butchered him. She butchered him into eight fresh meat cuts.

Was it a sin to kill someone who was already dead?

Knowing that her arms could do no more, she fell against the wall. 'Why God? Why? Why do the same things keep happening to me? What is wrong with me? Why don't you ever show mercy? WHY?' she said out aloud.

She drew the knife up to her stomach with both hands. She had no one to linger on with life for now. A burning sting melted into her skin, munching its way to the bone. As though God had heard her plea, her body was emptied of soul before the tip of the blade even brushed the front of her blood-soaked dress.

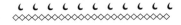

Guilt fuzzed around Daud in a shadow as he gulped down yet another mug of liquor. The table before him was scattered with mugs. It tasted bitter, fizzy and foul. He hadn't had the money to buy the drinks but Elijah and Ethan had let him in, seeing that he was in distress. Today was the first time he did not notice their agitating feminine mannerisms.

Daud was glued to his seat, flapping half way on the table like fabric, whilst the boys just kept ordering more booze for him.

He didn't want anymore, he had had enough. He never wanted to feel so bloated and sludgy again.

'Another one for the gentleman,' shouted Ethan.

Daud shook his head reluctantly. 'No, no more please.' Everything floated menacingly around him.

'Just one more won't do you any harm. You're a man now,' Elijah said. He gently pulled Daud by the hips back into his seat.

'But, but this is not the kind of man I want to be,' Daud said, his senses not completely vanished. 'I don't want to be like him!'

Understanding very well to whom Daud was referring, Elijah tried to console him. 'Don't worry. This is a medicine. It will take your anger away,' he said. He forced open Daud's clamped jaw and poured in some more alcohol.

Soon enough Daud was drugged. Totally blacked out. The two young men slung him on their shoulders, his legs paddling behind him like logs of jelly. They walked a few paces in the smelly alleyways until they reached a spot where no one could see anything. Daud gurgled in an effervescing stance.

'Put him on this,' Ethan said as he kicked a few idle mud bricks to form a worktop.

They lay him down on his stomach, his legs dangling from the edge of the platform, and pulled his futah[1] down.

'Me first,' Elijah said. He thrusted himself into Daud.

'Now my turn,' Ethan hissed, shuddering with excitement.

Daud was not completely knocked out. He knew what was happening. It was disgusting, but he could not do a thing to stop it. He cried, wept with helplessness at how he was being used. The three grotesque shadows on the walls horrified him.

The next morning, two of the shadows were found dead in

the obscure corner.

The third shadow was running away from its body as fast as it could.

<hr>

[1] Yemeni male attire.

Interconnectivity

BLAST!

The trumpet roars, deafening every created being with its force. Twists of iridescent green air windsweep everything in its course.

Souls, upon the sudden eruptive vibrations, urge their physical bodies to react to the summons. People, one by one sit up. The mud of their graves slides off into a damp murky pile at their feet. Covered in tufts of soil, dust and insects, their eyes are turned upwards, watching their souls soar above them.

Seraphiel, the angel whose divine occupation is to propel the horn, puffs up his golden cheeks again. His glowing mouth gusts violently into the trumpet.

Upon the second blast, everyone rises to their feet, ready to witness the Resurrection. They stand wearily, since this day will be fifty thousand years long. Naked and sweaty, they cluster in a rugged whir under the throne. The sun's blazing heat scorches their skins clinically white- it stands firing at its zenith. A gradual personal sea of perspiration looms within seconds. For some the level is to the ankles, others to the waist, but overall the majority just try to prevent themselves from drowning in it.

Mountains rumble and shake into dust with the force of a belching sneeze.

Two scrolls, miles long, are rolled out into a carpet for each person. The Inquisition regarding Great and Small is uniform. Each body trembles violently, shaking the hairs out from their follicles. Blood froths and buzzes.

Andrew stepped on one end of the hair-thin Sirat Bridge. He places a foot on it, it was sharper than a sword. He could barely see it. Would he slide into the Gardens, the vineyards? Could he be doubted? Hesitantly, he follows with his other foot. In an instant, calculated to be a millionth of a second, he is in crawling position. Too scared to look down, and terrorised by having to stand up, he looks back to the edge, but it is miles away. He panics. Making every effort to move forward cautiously and carefully, so as not to falter into the boiling red fireball, he slithers along. The task is outrageously difficult, it is like hauling one's body weight across a single strand of hair, sharp enough to slice right through you.

Breathlessness. Andrew closes his eyes for a second, letting the oxygen reach his numb brain.

When he opened his eyes and felt a little better, he was suddenly slammed down into the fangs of the fire.

As he recalls the Day, another tear splashes onto his face. It feels like the lash of a leather whip poking itself into his eye socket. The flesh of his skin peels off and sinks into the flames. Spirits maintain their existence in his veins, hissing their rough, corrugated tongues into his ears with each scorch they feel. His eyes overflow like egg-white onto his cheeks.

But this is not the worst of it, because he can't even scream. Each time he does, scalding toxic water burns his body into a puddle of blood. He attempts to console himself with food. He was hungry for days. He picked up a walnut from a nearby table in desperation. Andrew chewed it, and with each movement he felt the nugget enlarging, sprouting thorns into his cheeks. It grew so large and painful that he could not even spit it out. His jaw snapped. Nevertheless, this was less horrifying than the burning garments of fire which blackened him blacker than any coal.

Andrew knows that he must remain here for quite some

time until he is fully equipped to be brought forward again for a trial. He must become accustomed to the hypnotic rhythm of howls and screeches which stand ready to jump at him with each blink. Once his sentence is over, he can abandon this abyss in Hell and look forward to an orchard in Heaven.

Lengthy hopes are caused by two factors: ignorance and love of Earth. Andrew is determined to pass the Repentance Test second time round, and glide straight into Paradise on the Sirat Bridge, instead of falling into the gulf of this doomed place: a palace for the profligate.

Unfortunately, this is yet another aspiration, its only advantage being that it keeps him going. Time has already run out.

Chapter 10

The ride to the palace was one which was bundled in silence – not because each girl didn't want to find out about the others or engage in friendly talk, but because all of them were nervous of the new path laid out in front of them. Huddled women, sharing each other's body heat, all stared at the jiggling floor quietly as if they wanted it to open up and suck them in.

The recent events largely confused Sara. Was it Fate that they were removed from the ship, or bad luck? Could the prospects be analysed positively or negatively? The brightest advantage of the entire matter was that they were still in Yemen. Maybe they could meet Mother and Daud again. She bit her lip nervously. She felt a load in her chest become unbearably heavy as she recalled memories of her loved ones.

Mimmy sighed in her slumber, nuzzling into Sara's chest as far as her head could dig into it.

The morning was warm, thin clouds stretched lethargically in the sky. Tension gurgled on the edges of her eyelids. Images of Helena's face and Daud's face bobbed up and down in the river of turmoil crashing downstream towards her. She looked up. There was no water in the sky. The resentment, she admitted, was not owed to the fact that she was going to the palace, but because they could not share the moment with her family. Her thoughts were cluttered with a burst of fresh anticipation. They were going to a palace! A real palace, instead of the dream castles she imagined nestling in pink-purple clouds in the sky. She wondered how many rooms there would be, what kind of clothes people would wear. Even if she was to be a maid surrounded with such exquisite beauty, she didn't mind: day by day would fascinate her.

Eventually the carriage stopped. It was a bright, glowing day, which served to temporarily numb the young maidens' memories. The carriage driver told them to get off the carriage and stand in a line. As Sara was getting off she noticed how pale and soft the sand beneath her feet was. Her feet felt as if they were being caressed by soft, feathery cotton balls. Mimmy had observed the same quality and was busy swapping fistfuls of the sand from one hand to the other. Sara wriggled her toes in the luxurious bedding that extended vastly around the colossal monument that stared down at them.

The high structured marble beamed in the sunlight, and the huge wooden sea-green window shutters and doors carved in delicate fretwork provided a striking contrast to the bleached building. From where they were standing, the palace glistened like the inside of an oyster shell lying on the shore of Aden's beaches, every so often being moistened by drizzles of seawater. Here, the drizzles were golden looms of air wrapping themselves around the most prominent tower in the building. A lush green canopy surrounded the outskirts of the area in a steady patch of shade. Vegetation appeared to have been glued together, unmistakeably resembling a wonderful design.

'Follow me,' a husky voice said in thick Arabic, abruptly jolting them out of the mystical daze which all of the girls were enveloped in. The voice belonged to a woman in her middle ages but very well kept. Pads of fat covered her well. Her face was square, and possessed rounded cheeks relaying clues to her actual age. She wore a long violet gown which flapped gracefully with every step she took, coupled with pointed leather mules which accentuated her authoritative gait. It was blatantly obvious that she was not one of the royals, but she was not dressed or had mannerisms like a maid either. She was 'something in between,' and very well respected since it could be deduced from the upright way she chose to walk. 'Chose to walk' because Sara knew that no one walked so stiffly as if they had a pole fastened onto their spines unless they had an audience.

They followed the lady in an orderly line, like a flapping tail. 'Shusk! Shusk! Shusk!' The sand fluttered as it flew up into the air with each of Mimmy's little kicks.

'Stop it Mimmy! You'll get us into trouble,' Sara said. She grabbed Mimmy's little paw in hers. As they drew closer to the door of the palace, Sara felt a layer of sweat squirt onto her back. She had to conceal the fact she was a Jew and she had to change her name. She knew that in Aden it did not matter if you were a Jew or Muslim or Christian – they were all believers of monotheism, the Abrahamic faith. But since the finger-pointing episode on the ship, Sara was not so sure. If she wanted to stay with Mimmy she would have to ensure every little detail about herself was carefully planned, and perhaps more importantly, carefully concealed. A drop of sweat trickled down her forehead as she hurriedly tried to think of a new identity. Her mind went blank. It was coincidental how under times of pressure it always managed to do that.

'Right, I want all of you to wait here whilst I fetch the manager. He will allocate you to where you have to go, your duties and your salaries,' she said, making such wild gestures with her hands that it almost seemed as if she would flap up to the ceiling like a bird. These people were different – noticeably different – to the people of Aden. In Aden, people were short, dark and extremely good tradesmen. The men spoke with emotional gestures but the women always stayed respectfully quiet. Here, the women seemed to have equal status to the men – or was it that they possessed the same qualities? Sara didn't know.

'Sara,' whispered Mimmy, 'I have to go wee!' She twisted her legs around one another like twine looking quite desperate.

'Just a minute, you'll have to hold on, I'll have to ask the lady. You must keep it in Mimmy. We'll be punished if you don't!'

'I caaaan't!' Mimmy said. She was now hopping about and urinating a small puddle on the floor.

The other girls gaped at Mimmy.

Sara was horrified. 'Oh no, what have you done!' She tried to wipe it clean with a rag from her bundle. Her face went beetroot red as she felt the sixteen eyes glaring at her every swipe.

'Here, take this,' one of the younger girls said. She handed her a cloth.

'Thanks.' Sara noticed the girl's brilliant black kohl smeared eyes. She chased the fluorescent soggy mess on the floor as if her life depended on it.

A pair of footsteps were audible, clacking in synchronisation. They stopped, right beside where Sara was washing the puddle with the rag.

'What are you doing?'

Sara looked up to find it was the same one who had told them to wait.

Almost choked by electrified nerves, Sara stood up. 'I'm sorry Syeddati. My sister just needed the toilet and suddenly it came out on the floor. There was no one around to ask and she, being a child, could not wait.' Her lips continued to tremble even after she finished the sentence.

Mimmy peered out from behind Sara's back as Sara realised what she had just done. She'd given away that they were sisters!

'How disgusting,' the man sneered. He was lean, but curiously occupied a heavy tread. His eyes were like black slits in his face, accompanying his voice which was sudden and sharp, like a clap of thunder. 'Where is the youngster?'

Mimmy jostled behind Sara as a barrier.

The manager walked round to catch sight of her. 'Why this child is no more than six years old! How did this happen? In fact these two are too young for Sheikh Khalil's employment.'

'What shall we do then?' the lady said.

'Maybe we can ask Sheikh Atif if he needs them for any of his chores.'

'You are correct.'

'All of you follow me,' the supervisor ordered. 'Rawia, you take care of these two.'

Sara watched like an orphaned kitten as she was separated from the other girls. They left, in single file in an ant trail, behind the giant strides of the supervisor.

'What are your names?' Rawia said, speaking fondly for the first time, her stiff mannerisms suddenly dissolving.

'I am Arwa, and this is my sister Miriam.' Sara said this with as much confidence as that of a typical liar, an actor. It was not fear but fantasy which was responsible for the strange development in her. She was mesmerised by the palace, the most beautiful thing she had ever seen. Unsurprisingly, its magic had taken possession of her quite soon, and she felt compelled to secure her sister's future here in respectable employment. She would make her owners proud, it would be her life-long ambition.

'How old are you?'

'I am fifteen and she is six.'

'Usually the girls that come for Sheikh Khalil's employment are much older and mature. How did you two find your way here?'

'We were sold by our father.'

'Sold by your father?'

She nodded, the pain of reality tightened around her chest like a suffocating metal corset.

'Don't you worry, you'll be safe and happy here. I've been over here for two decades. You know, this palace is owned by Sheikh Khalil, he is a widower, with a young son Atif. That boy is a gallant young boy, at least he used to be until his mother died. Since then he has sobered up a bit. It's as if he has been forced into a cage of silence and coldness. He doesn't get along well with his father that much.' Rawia ranted on like a buzzing bee. 'I'll make sure that you stay in Atif's employment. With Sheikh Khalil, there's no saying what he might indulge in next!'

'Indulge in *next*?' Sara said.

'He is an epitome of the seven deadly sins. He never used to be like this. He was very noble, and generous. Everyone respected him. Light shone from him like a glamorous cloak. His face gleamed with happiness. His shadow was glazed permanently with kindness. But then overnight he changed. Some say his rivals have practiced black magic on him. Others say that he was always like this, putting a show on for society and driving Syeddati Noha, his wife, insane. But I don't believe a word of it. I knew that man was as good as gold. Patient as a turtle overturned on its shell. Overnight he just snapped.' She paused in her praise when she realised that she may have released too much information to a child. It had been a long time since she had made a real connection with someone.

Sara tried to gulp all this information in. Was she in a mad house? A palace of mystery and madness?

'Now come along. You both must bathe and get cleaned before you are taken before the Sheikh. He'll know what to do with you.'

Both of them followed obediently, their stomachs growling loudly in front of them like pets.

'You must be hungry,' Rawia said. 'It'll all come, but you must be perfectly clean first!'

She led them into a small room with a hammam[1] at the back. The room was not as densely accumulated with gold as the rest of the building, but it was exquisite in its own way.

Secretly, Sara was thankful for being led here. It was a life that she had always wanted to be a part of, and now she was a character in her custom made dream castle.

[1] Bathroom

Chapter 11

Everything shone at her, reflecting long striated shimmers on the decorative marble walls. The hand painted tiles smothered on the floor were so highly glossed that Sara was amazed she didn't glide on the polish and slam straight into the calligraphic wall. The even shot vertical reflections straight up at the ceiling. Curved accessories juxtaposed the geometric tile patterns, giving an overall glaring effect. At the centre of the room was a huge rose pool with gold engravings similar to that of the wall sconces which lit up the room. Beside it was a table with rolled up cloths and silver bottles arranged neatly in a pyramid. The atmosphere was very well created. She didn't know what she was looking at, but she knew that she was struck by the beauty of it.

They followed Rawia's lead, and groped their way through the maze of walls and staircases. Sara had observed how the entire palace was bathed in natural daylight, which flooded each and every space. The sheer embroidered voiles manipulated the sunlight so that each corner or corridor received a variable quantity, just enough to mask the glare which currents to the rest of the world outside the window. But not their world anymore. They were a part of *this* one. This Oriental Wonderland.

Rawia deserted them in a massive room which had no practicality. She removed Mimmy's outer garment which was riddled with streaks of coffee, sand and urine. At home, they only washed their hair once a month, when Andrew and Daud brought the water in the large mud bowls when it was their turn in the neighbourhood. She didn't know whether she was happy or sad, thankful or resentful to be part of this historic vogue. The initial optimism began to dissolve. Fizz. A feeling of uneasiness haunted Sara, heightening, demanding attention as usual. Everything was too perfect, too man made. She recalled the entertaining pleasure of spotting a butterfly roam their ruddy walls, sailing a ribbon of *natural* atmosphere into their home. The rare fascination of sighting a baboon on an expedition for firewood, drawing away from it at the time, but then having days of amusement talking about the incident later. She recalled the comfort of seeing an undernourished tree with its scraggly bark, bravely supporting their life against drought. Nature strength was her motivation.

Mimmy stepped into the huge bowl and Sara poured splashes of warm, bubbly rose scented water onto the excited child. She paddled about splattering bright peach and yellow petals everywhere. A healthy pride and vitality radiated awkwardly out from her seemingly malnutritioned body. Rawia left them long violet coloured dresses to change into, and after they both were scrubbed clean, they greedily slipped into their new garments, which were starched stiff. In the reflection on the tiles they resembled dolls, a large size and a compact size, bought from the same brand.

Breakfast at the palace began with prayers from the Qur'an and everyone then filled their bowls modestly. Despite their apparent poverty, all the girls usurped new personas, dressed in clothes similar to that of Sara and Mimmy and delicately groomed. It was evident that each girl had paid special attention to her appearance that morning.

Sara had never seen so much food in her life, richly coloured fruits whose skins shined so vibrantly that it seemed as if they had been polished along with the ornaments; golden honey glazed baklava pastries; trays bulged with beads of green fruit; shanks of juicy meat and piles of soft, wheaty bread. The courses were laid out in a magnificent presentation, captivating the stomachs of those who stared at it. The combined aroma was that of a feast. Not a single girl knew how or where to begin.

The eight girls who arrived that morning were seated in a linear layout, with seats in front of them empty. Unable to resist the divinity that was displayed seductively before them, they began. They wore faces of relief as they munched the food freely. Each ate differently; some chewed each mouthful to the extent that it would dissolve on their tongues, others just bit the mouthful to size and swallowed it with haste.

Sara bit into a baklava pastry, the honey clinging to her lips and the pastry obstinately latching itself onto it in a wafery scatter. Embarrassed, she kneeled forward and swept a glance around to see if any of the others looked the same. They didn't.

'After you have finished breakfast girls you will be allocated your tasks.' Rawia paused in her animated attitude as if she wanted everyone to notice her new change of clothes. It had to be admitted, she played her part very well.

'Arwa and Miriam, you will accompany me.' She whooshed out of the room, her skirts ballooning more than ever.

Sara wiped her mouth clean with the tablecloth. Her tummy was stretched to full capacity and felt like she had an army of babies waiting inside.

'No silly, this is for you to wipe your hands and mouth with,' whispered the kind girl who had lent her the cloth when Mimmy wet herself in the courtyard. She lent over more towards Sara. 'This is just to protect the table,' she said as she pointed at the huge cloth draped over the table.

'My name is Arwa, what is yours?'

'I'm Lulu.'

'Lulu?'

'Yes.'

'What does that mean?'

'Pearls.'

'How beautiful.' She realised how much the name clashed with the girl's appearance. She was a beauty alright, a Black Bedouin Beauty.

They were interrupted by the squawky supervisor. He entered with his chin facing the ceiling that it was a wonder his neck did not snap and his head fall backwards. 'Everyone apart from these two young ones will come with me.' He cast his hooded eyes upon the nervous faces, which eventually rested on Lulu. 'You, how old are you?'

'Fourteen sir.'

'Fourteen?' Her curvaceous looks deceived everyone. 'Then you are far too immature for the task. You will stay with these two and see what task Sheikh Atif has for you to do.' He was silent for a moment, gazing into Lulu's face as if to reconfirm his decision, then vanished with the speed of a fly being squatted.

Both Lulu and Sara (now Arwa) were glad. At least they had each other as friends, someone to share their feelings with in the Exotic Kingdom.

Lulu was a tribal sheikh's daughter, she revealed to Sara that night. In the eyes of her community, her father was privileged and respected, and his opinion overrode all other considerations. Unlike the palace sheikhs, tribal sheikhs were appointed as the leader of the tribe, bestowed with a power and responsibility without owning any land or riches. Lulu used to roam the undulating landscape with her tribe, surviving on the piece of land that she stood on. What astonished Sara the most was learning that despite Lulu's primitive lifestyle, she received an education and lessons in mannerisms similar to that of girls in a palace harem. She could even do book-keeping! Lulu's father adored her, and supported her to evolve into a smart, challenging and honourable woman.

It was his logic that Lulu did not comprehend.

One day, her brother injured another sheikh's son in a hunting parade, by accident. He ran home, terrified of being the trigger of a potential blood feud. Lulu's father was silent, and decided to settle the potential danger to his tribe through a payment of five women. Marriage loops everyone together. However, the only insurance the other sheikh wanted was Lulu, and she was given away, thinking that she would cultivate peace. To her horror, the enemy tribe leader sold her off to the ship. Lulu had no idea where her family could be, whether they were killed and destroyed under the justification of 'honour,' or if her people were dispersed altogether. She felt that 'honour,' in the hands of wrong people was a feeble excuse for the arrogance whose sole role was to divide people.

Sara agreed.

'Come along,' Rawia said, leading the three timid girls towards the younger Sheikh. 'Make sure you stand straight, eyes focused on the floor and agree to whatever he tells you to do. He is a nice young man but sometimes he just swims in silence.' She chattered on, all three of them listened carefully, including Mimmy.

Huge exotic sceneries dramatised the background of the white slats of the wall. They were an image to behold. Surprise-laden dream houses covered blank walls with colour bursting mosaics, tropical forests and lush flowers. The palace dreamt itself out of Yemen, flying away from the greying mountain plateaux, distancing itself from the sullen camels and honking geese weaving through the sand, escaping from a landscape which had neither a beginning nor an end. Fountains strewn with brilliant shocks of pink and orange petals replaced the swaying palm groves. Silver, golden and brass sickles on turquoise padded walls camouflaged the barrenness of the view outside. Ample space and peace, seat of flower petals deafened out the ramshackle rumble on the streets. A captivating composition, the palace was constructed with slabs of imagination, desire and, curiously, a fear.

They stopped outside a double door, covered with gold and wooden fretwork. Rawia rung a tiny silver bell concealed artistically in a groove beside the door. 'Ching, Ching, Ching.' A muffled ring came from inside in response to let them enter. Rawia pushed the huge door open and all three of them stepped in, in one single movement, staring obediently at the floor. For the first time since she had arrived, Sara was aware of how out of place her tattered shoes with their wisping threads looked on the decorative floor. They gave it a snaggly, battered look.

'So you are the three young girls who can not attend to my father,' a young masculine voice said, speaking in sharp, crisp Arabic. His voice resonated from behind a tall desk in the corner of the room 'Well you shall be in my employment then.' His footsteps drew near, and stopped in front of Mimmy.

Mimmy looked up at this magnificent man, clad in a black and silver robe with a white head piece. There was a powerful silence which hovered around them for a moment. He took short sips of mint tea. His bronzed face glowed in a towering light. An expression of purity conjured itself as his vacant hand kept moving, saying his prayer beads with every second that passed. Soft, fresh fragrances enveloped him in a pillowcase.

Young Sheikh Atif sat in his office at the end of the corridor, which was surrounded with small rooms on either side. This position was central and he could keep a steady account of customers and tradesmen that visited. Sheikh Khalil, his father, had taught him the knack of being shrewd in business and had even taken the liberty of giving him lessons explaining how furniture layout coupled with body language could be a powerful tool in itself.

He resumed his seat casually at his desk again. 'You may look up now. If you stare any longer at the floor the patterns will come to life!'

Lulu and Sara raised their eyes slowly, realising the truth in the man's sarcasm.

'I am Sheikh Atif, son of Sheikh Khalil. I understand you shall be in my service. What can you do?'

Silence.

'I'm asking you a question.'

Sara raised her eyes to meet his. Sheikh Atif was a handsome young man with a strong jaw line and dark hair which complemented his nutty skin colour. He was tall and broad shouldered, muscles hugged him in the right places giving a clue that he was an athlete. He looked like nut paste with the most gorgeous large eyes Sara had ever seen. His eyes were a curious shade of brown with tinges of green radiating out from the centre. Cloisters of thick black lashes framed the eyes in a sort of nest, which possessed a mysterious quality of appearing to brew constantly within themselves.

He stared back at her, waiting for a response.

113

'I can sew dolls,' she finally said, forgetting to mention that she also specialised in beauty treatments.

'Dolls. What kind of dolls?'

'Small decorative dolls that Father used to sell in the market.'

'Interesting. Do you enjoy it?' He fingered an ugly grass vase on his desk. It was shaped like a duck. The reed boys made better handicrafts in Rawdah Village, they were more skilful at their work.

'I suppose.'

'And this is your sister. She resembles you very much.' His attention diverted very quickly to Lulu. 'And you, what can you do?'

'I can embroider Sir. I am also able to do a little gardening,' Lulu said. She did not inform him that she could do book-keeping or cook, she wanted to remain with her new friends. She clutched the sides of her thighs so he would not realise that her knees were jittering.

Atif longed to be an expert in his trade, and many agreed that he was, but his self-assertion and sudden tantrums of defiance were not unknown to those who visited. His body reflected his lifestyle, his prosperous upbringing, but his mind was deeply scarred. Firmly rooted in his beliefs, he was evidently weakened from time to time by an inner battle he fought with himself. This was projected to the public in the form of sudden decisions, swapping of tone or just plain fidgeting.

Sheikh Atif stood up. Sara saw how he stood with his head slightly lowered, immediately placing him on a pedestal of humbleness and respect. He was well sculpted, his broad shoulders draped with his luxurious flowing black robe. She blinked. His orchard eyes turned rocky, steep and hard, and fused with a dash of violet and indigo. A chemical reaction occurred in his eye balls.

'All three of you shall make dolls. Each lady that comes to this palace and visits my father's tower, you shall make a doll dressed like her. At the end of each month we shall have them displayed and you will receive your salaries.' He spoke in a series of fits.

Startled at the sudden shift in his soft tone, the three girls observed his face.

'Rawia will attend to your fabric needs and materials. She will also pay your salary. Once we have a library, then we'll show him.' For a split second he was both present and absent at the same time. He stopped, as if realising that his manner was confusing his startled young visitors.

'I'm sure that you will enjoy yourselves and your time here. By Allah, we treat our workers with the same hospitality as we would with any of our guests,' he said softly. 'You may leave now!'

As they marched in a uniform fashion out of the room, Atif caught Rawia in the doorway. 'Rawia, I don't want any of these girls to be exposed to my father. You must make sure of that always.' He lowered his face to hers so that she could catch the confidentiality of the matter.

Nodding, Rawia hushed them all out of the room, and the door shut with a loud, powerful thud.

Lulu's Loss

Lulu stood tearfully, trembling outside the seven enormous gates. Once she had entered, this would be her eternal abode. Crowds of souls bundled together, shaking in harmony with nervousness. Fear cleaved to them in a thunder storm – each person trying to keep dry from their own lightning. It turned out that death and birth were the same thing. It was only the presence that mattered, and now her Fallen Presence was here.

The hot, splintered fumes of the fire lashed out towards them from one of the gates. It blew so fiercely that everyone felt a prick of the white achy sparks darkening their skins. A woman in the crowd outside the third gate screamed. She was being dragged on her face so Lulu could not see it.

Hell was a world. Massive bunches of maroon and black hills formed the landscape. As the gate opened, the hills got up. The maroon ones were hideous gorging scorpions and the black ones were uncoiling and slithering menacingly towards the fire; colossal blown-up monsters.

'Forgive me, Forgive me! I am a murderer.' It was the same woman who was being dragged on her face. Arrows were protruding from every part of her flesh- they grew out of her like body parts. For a split second, Lulu thought she recognised the voice. But her suspicion was soon drowned out as she heard a blood curdling shriek from her queue.

Why hadn't she acted rationally? Why had it not occurred to her that she would be forgiven? After all, He is the most Merciful – He promised mercy for repentance. Who was she to take the matter into her own hands?

She stepped forward, her turn was coming nearer. The step was not an eager one, but a confident one- as though having to accept all that was being thrown in her direction. She could feel the blood belching in her heart menacingly. With each step forward, the squelches got louder.

Nearer to the gate, the sinners were separated into three rows. Lulu was in the third. Once she entered:

The people of the first row repeatedly thrust weapons into themselves. Their bones snapped loudly.

The people in the second row kept sipping poison for eternity whilst being scorched by the hissing flames.

And in the third row, they were hurled with such intensity over the tip of the entrance that they kept falling and falling, consistently, until they reached the base of the bottomless pit.

If there was one.

Still suspending downwards with unparalleled speed, she heard the gate clang shut many, many centuries later. The echo deafened her ears as she continued spiralling below.

The Intervening Years

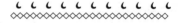

Dhul Hijjah 1740

Dear Mother,

Look! I can write now. I am learning fast. My Arabic tutor says soon I can write full page letter to you. Mimmy is fine- we spend much time together, Mimmy, I and Lulu. Syed Hamid said if I practice I go far.

I shall write again soon.

Your daughter,
Sara

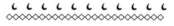

Muharram 1740

Dear Mother,

Since last week I have learnt many more words. Syed Hamid was very pleased with me this week. I showed him my first letter to you. He said I am ideal student. I made sure that I didn't sign it as my name before showing him though.

Yesterday I saw Sheikh Atif again. He came to collect the dolls we made. He seemed worried, I do not know why. His eyes were crawling in fear. He is nice man, he has educated all of his staff. May his God bless him. I miss you both. Tell Daud we are fine. No need to worry. He should spend his time taking care of you now.

Your ever loving daughter,
Sara

Dear Mother,

Mimmy has grown very much now. I have taught her how to embroider- she is learning slowly. Lulu teaches her also. Lulu is my best friend. I would be lost without her. She helps me bring up Mimmy. I tell her almost everything and I think she tells me too.

I hope Daud and Deborah are together and happy. I hope you are with them and away from Father. I pray for health Mother, take special care of yourself.

Today something bad happened. Murad did not come to collect the dolls so I stood outside without my purdah waiting for him. One of the male secretaries come instead and he saw me without my purdah. His face changed colour. His skin changed purple. I think it was because I broke the custom. I leapt back into the room and shut the door. Rawia came later and warned me not to do the same again. 'What must be hidden should be kept hidden,' she said. That was close. If I was sacked what could I do for Mimmy?

Anyways take care.
Your devoted daughter
Sara

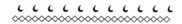

Safar 1746

Dear Mother,

I am very happy today. I saw a dream. We were in a big house, all of us, Mimmy, Daud, you, Deborah, me and Lulu and we played in the grass. The garden was a jewel garden- all colours you can imagine. I could even smell the flowers when I woke up. Then there was a knock on the door, I opened it and there was a black room. Inside there was a black nest, and on it lay a crow which had the face of Sheikh Atif. The red eyes looked at me.

Then I woke up.

I told Syed Hamid and he laughed. Lulu nudged me, so I did not mention the black crow to him. Next month we may be starting poetry.

May you always remain happy,

Yours faithfully,
Sara

Ramadan 1747

Dear Mother,

Everyone is busy for Ramadan. I woke up for Sahri and break my fast too. It is very easy. I feel I work faster. Mimmy can't manage though- I think she is not used to working on empty stomach. She is weak. Rawia gave us honey to strengthen her system, it was generous of her. Honey must be very cheap here since they use a lot of it. They use it for everything- for face creams to soap bars. I am struck by the kindness in the palace. Is it because they are genuinely nice or just that they have extra to share? I cannot conclude. If you have more I suppose it should be easier to share.

I am grateful for my life here. I wish you could join us. Mimmy remembers you sometimes too. I think she misses Father more, even though I tell her not to.

Your one and only,
Sara

Shawwal 1747

Dear Mother,

Lulu has taught me many things, but I am afraid I am still not like her. I desire the peace she is at with herself. I worry all the time about you. She helps me- I have learnt how to pray from her. I fell much better now. Syed Hamid also taught me some Surahs which I practice every night. Mimmy gets into trouble because she forgets to complete her tasks for him. We help her to do so.

And yes, I feel more like 'Arwa' now. Please do not mind. I prefer to be called that since this is my identity in the palace.

I love you always,
Arwa

Dhul-Qa'ada 1749

Dear Mother,

Since the morning I have not been feeling well. I wrote my first poem, 'Flawless Human.' We all try to be one- me too. I hope it will benefit Mimmy- I am noticing a dangerous change in her. We don't get along that much anymore. I spent weeks on the poem. Syed Hamid said it was extremely well written and should be commended. I wish you could have seen the basket of fruits he rewarded me with.

I wish you could have seen my poem.

I wish you could have read just one letter.

I shall ask Mimmy to draw a picture of the gift for you.

One day you might just see it.

One day we might just meet.

Your forever loving,
Arwa

Chapter 12

A decade later...

The routine of the palace generated a rumble which lasted all day long. A thick influx of coffee beans and textiles jammed the usually silent courtyards for quality control; tradesmen shuffled in and out throughout the day, bringing perfume oils and other lucrative goods for wholesale agreements.

Many servants and administrative workers served their employment with a few, short breaks for prayers. Keeping their eyes resolutely magnetised to the ground, the servants constituted a theatre of their own. They blathered about anything and everything, sometimes even invented scandals for one another to escape the surliness of the palace.

Atif tended to remain at his desk at the end of the corridor, executing business feasibilities single-handedly. It was unfortunate that his father, his teacher, did not involve himself anymore. Ever since he had realised his son's ability to handle the baggage for him, he retired openly to his passions. Khalil claimed he 'mistrust my own self. A freshly educated mind, new ideas would reap higher rewards than my old fashioned ones.' And so, he shed the load onto Atif, spending his days in anticipation of tasty evenings in his private tower.

The tall slanted tower was situated in the back of the courtyard, and away from the main foundation of the palace. The stone it was constructed with provided a dark inky silhouette to the building which appeared to have a hulking shadow after dusk.

During the day the tower remained increasingly inanimate, deported from movement, sound or life altogether. Then, at night time, the whippet thin creases in the shutters of the windows would relish in colourful cone shaped glints and blinding gleams until dawn, when the presence of the sun executed the livid flashes until the following evening.

At first, Sara considered that the palace was indifferent to any extreme of weather due to its sturdy marble structure. It was uncomfortable accepting that the basic fundamentals of food and shelter did not demand any form of attention. Instead, it was the Ilb tree and coffee plantations which took the priority concern. The ugly, thorny bristle-bush tree, which evolved into gruesome batches on the highland plains, thrived on cool weather. The loss of Ilb was most feared since the sparse fruits and flowers were the prime ingredients for honey, and the trunk was used for construction purposes. In Rawda, the only use the villagers found for the tree was to collect its thick blade-like leaves to use as fodder for the animals. Whereas the hot weather was preferred to the cold due to the chaos the winds inflicted on the villagers' lifestyles, the palace depended on the Indian Ocean's monsoon winds drizzling their tonics of rain into the long throats of coffee and Ilb plants.

Here in the palace, this logic was twisted. The palace and the village were like night and day.

Sara melted into her new life with comfort, from a usual dreamy spectator called Sara to a hardworking Arwa. Progressively she had found herself converting to Islam. It was easier. She had not just converted for the sake of practicality, but she reasoned that this was the most purposeful as well. Her spirit did not starve this way. However, she did not influence Mimmy to adapt to the new level of purity she discovered. For Mimmy, it would be a personal choice. So she continued educating Mimmy of what she could recall of Helena's Jewish teachings, secretly, even when Lulu was out of earshot. Maybe a spark of fear haunted her for resuming Mimmy's Jewish lessons, but she sincerely believed that faith was a condition of the heart. And Mimmy's heart was Mimmy's choice.

The girls lived in a huge white room, pure as a newborn life, which overlooked the secretive tower so that they could see who entered and who left. Sewing dolls had become a hobby for all three of them. Arwa and Lulu did most of the sewing while Mimmy would stand at the window giving accurate descriptions of the girls that went in. Arwa never missed a detail. Whether it was a delicate and worried looking girl, or whether she had a crescent of curls stealing down her forehead or whether she had an awkwardness of posture, Arwa implanted the dolls with the spirit of the girls. The robes were the easy part, colourful cloths, with an incredible sliding ability on the wearers skins embroidered and appliquéd in tiny versions. Lulu expertly embroidered the dresses to an exact resemblance. Rawia provided them with fabrics which looked like cut pieces from the costumes that the girls wore themselves. Often, the girls wondered how Rawia managed to find exact templates and crafting aids, but they didn't think about it much since she was (in a way) the lady of the house.

As promised, at the end of every month they received their salaries. The white and gold spying outlet was their home; meals, extra orders and their games all happened in their room. They even had a real backgammon set made of pure wood (at home, Daud had scratched out a backgammon game on the floor with a fine twig and Sara had collected pebbles from beside the mosque to use as counters).

Occasionally Sheikh Arif came to collect the dolls himself instead of sending a servant boy or one of the eunuchs. Grudgingly he picked them up one by one and put them into the golden basket, which was sent ritually for the collection of dolls on a weekly basis.

Murad, an orphan whom the palace had adopted, arrived to gather the dolls. He was a type of Family Slave, running errands for everyone and just about anyone. Ironically he did not have a family, so he considered everyone as an extended member of his own. He believed that this was the best way to set up his own family – Allah, he believed, would reward him with a virtuous soul mate. Over the years he had evolved into a tall chiselled frame, impressively muscular and rapaciously lusty. His forearms were broad and bronzed, coated with a sheer layer of dark brown silky hair. When he moved, his powerful strides escalated the overall impact as his firm fists monotonously brushed each of his modelled thighs. A trail of hearts clinked behind him at the site of each of his footprints. The females fancied him, and the males respected him. It was expected that he would train for the army.

For the girls he was a daily support, a looking glass into life outside the palace. He gave them elaborate descriptions, and captivated Mimmy the most with his stories, who had had the least exposure. He reminded them of the erupting pavements of soil, the smell of the dust, the kiss of the sun and the bustle of the suq. They appreciated his knack for detail, it was a part of the day to look forward to. And more importantly, it was a diversion from the mystery of the forbidden tower.

Lulu and Arwa often wondered why young sprouting girls not much older than themselves went to the tower – it was a very strange practice. But they never asked, afraid that they would be beheaded and boiled, like in the series of adventures in 'A Thousand and One Nights.' Maybe Sheikh Khalil owned a factory much bigger than Atif's to produce woven fabrics. Maybe they were his wives and daughters, or both. Maybe he had a theatre of entertainment for his rich friends. They agreed it was better for them to ignore any assumptive concerns.

So they never found out.

Until Lulu met her fate.

Ten years of friendship plucked out in one go.

It all began early one morning when a eunuch brought the news that one of Sheikh Khalil's flower maidens had run away and he needed replacements to decorate the rooms in his tower immediately. The news swept through the palace like a whip snaking through the air.

Lulu's eyes gleamed at the prospect of being able to see the inside of the tower. 'Arwa, this is our chance to find out what happens inside the tower!'

Sara raised her eyes from her sewing. 'Are you sure you want to be made into a puppet and put in Atif's collection?' she asked, her voice unexpectedly wincing for the first time.

'What?' Mimmy and Lulu looked to each other for an explanation. 'Oh, never mind,' Lulu said.

'Come on, Arwa, it'll be fun. We'll unravel the mystery once and for all!' Mimmy hovered around Sara like a hen pecking its feed.

'*You* are not going anywhere,' Sara stated firmly. 'If it doesn't concern you, why should you be involved? Be grateful that you are safe, happy, literate and living.'

The two standing girls laughed at the familiar eroded, eaten-away outlook Arwa had for things.

'Well, I don't know about you two, but I sure want to know what goes on inside there. I'm going to offer myself as a temporary flower maiden,' said Lulu, pumping with a venturing spirit.

Mimmy cast her eyes directly in line with Arwa's for approval. As expected, she got none. She was tired of being treated and ordered about by Arwa.

'Lulu I don't think you should go either - it might not be safe. We don't know what goes on in there and we've been watching it for a decade–'

'Precisely.'

'Lulu…. please….'

'Loosen up, Arwa. I'll be fine. I'll be back before Fajr payer. You know I never miss Fajr. I'll tell you what happens when I get back,' she said, shrugging her shoulders. She rummaged through her clothes to dress up appropriately. She drew out a sensuous lush cranberry robe, embroidered with a silver leaf pattern which she designed herself. Sheikh Khalil was a phantom figure whom they had all heard about, but never seen – she wanted to look her best in case she did meet him. Mimmy helped her dress.

'Anyone would think you were being prepared for your wedding,' Sara said, not lifting her head from the sewing, which was surprisingly keeping her attention focused that morning. Lulu's sudden determination opened the way for an alarming sensation which she had not encountered since she had been deserted by Andrew.

To accompany her cranberry dress, Mimmy plaited Lulu's ebony locks with a matching ribbon. They were salaried well enough to afford such accessories and fabrics. Instead of going to the suq, the suq was bought to them. Just before she left the room Sara got up to hug Lulu. 'Take care of yourself,' she whispered. Uncertainty wisped all over her face.

She appeared on the verge of adventure. 'I will,' she said. The pupils in her eyes flashed and her faced beamed a smile.

If only they could have captured that smile.

Then she left.

From the window, Mimmy and Sara watched her enter the tower, with a basket full of soft red and white petals. Even from the distance, the red dotted stains on the pollinated white petals were visible. She entered with two other girls who held the same kind of baskets stuffed with fragrant petals, imitating their stance the best that she could.

Sara stood rooted to the spot, a colony of stings scraping her back. Turning away, she wondered whether she had to create a model of Lulu, she was only the flower girl after all. She decided to make a little doll for Lulu as a present. Mimmy helped her, cutting the fabrics and threads to shape. Delicately, they got their crafted creation ready for Lulu's return, sprinkling it with shimmering sequins.

But she never came.

After Maghrib prayer, Sara got worried. They decided to wait a little longer. Time passed and Mimmy lit the wall sconces to lighten the heavy mood. Their function was to reduce the danger in the dark, the pressing concerns, but Sara felt that the uneven glows they threw around gave the atmosphere a further quality of eeriness.

"Mimmy, I think we should go and find Rawia."

If I had gone with her none of this would have happened, Mimmy thought to herself.

They put on their black veils and headed out to hunt for Rawia. They passed the rows of doors and weaved through the servants who were busy in their chores. From the windows they saw gardeners sprinkling an oily layer onto the mud, so that it would become too heavy for the dust storms expected to spray the dirt about. It was a last resort, since the anticipated rain squall didn't visit that season.

They spotted Rawia.

'Rawia! Rawia,' Sara exclaimed. 'Lulu went to do the flower arrangements in the tower… she's not been seen since!'

Rawia looked up at the girl's face, expressionless. It was not that she did not know what to tell the girl, it was *how* to tell her. 'My dear, it is past midnight now, the procession has started. She must be enjoying herself,' she said. The tip of her tongue blushed red.

'What?'

'You'll see her in the morning.'

Sara decided to investigate for herself.

It was not that Rawia approved of what happened in the tower. It was not that she didn't care. It was the fact that she knew she couldn't do anything about it. She looked away, the guilt enclosing her chest in batches of thorny twines. She should have warned them.

The truth kept Rawia from speaking any further.

But, Mimmy knew Lulu was safe. Mimmy knew that for sure. She was protected, penetrated, privileged. Often, when Arwa and Lulu were sleeping at night, she quietly slipped out of their room, treading into the forbidden lands. The force of desire did not come to her naturally, in actual fact the feeling stemmed after she was exposed to an apparent secrecy under her very nose. Soon it became unbearable in its touch, and she felt that she needed to be satisfied. She continued to keep this to herself.

Discontent with what Rawia told her to do, Sara ran out before the others could snap out of their silence. It was up to her. Lulu was her friend, her sister, her family. She couldn't lose yet *another* family member. She ran down the marble halls and wooden staircases in a fury that fired up inside of her. Why hadn't she stopped Lulu from leaving? Why? She should have been firm.

Mimmy sped after her sister. Mimmy had grown up watching the entertainment, the vivacious voyeurism. The thrill tingled her to her toes. There was nothing wrong with it – just that she had betrayed both Lulu and Arwa's trust when she crept out silently so she could taste a slice of the sensuality. Arwa's soul was from Rawda – the ruddy rubble slime, the raped landscape.

Sara swept through the blue glow of the courtyard, rose bush thorns pierced her flapping veil and shredded it. But nothing would stop her. Their defensive scent wafted after her. She finally approached the slanted tower, which was now brewing with motion. The warm smell of apple flavoured shisha hovered around the tower like a signal. She searched for the door – it was cleverly concealed under the tightly knotted branches of a date tree. White eunuchs let her in.

The iron door creaked open quite callously as she entered. The symptoms of danger were apparent: the isolated hallway was dark, but drenched in frankincense. Petal potion was used in tremendous quantity, so much so that it could even be tasted by naked eyeballs. Soft energetic beats of drums were heard, seeping down from the magnificent spiral staircase that stood before her. Maybe it is just a party. Maybe Lulu was enjoying herself. For a short, precise moment, she longed to be a part of it too.

Slowly and cautiously she made her way up the stairs, there were many, which was surprising, for why would a rich man like Sheikh Khalil climb these tediously and then go down them was beyond reason.

At the end of the spiral staircase sprint was a huge door, painted delicately and engraved with Arabic poetry. Authentic Islamic buildings included Arabic borders on edges, at the point before the ceiling turned into a wall. Sara read a bit of the calligraphy:

The Harem:
'Wrapped in petals she lies in her silent slumber
…Awaiting her turn to wake up tempation…'

The 'harem' was the part of a house set aside, secluded for women in the Arab world. Everyone knew that, Syed Hamid didn't need to teach her that. Separation of the sexes was fundamental to the Islamic household. Then what on earth was this description of the 'wake up temptation?' It sounded comic. People, she thought disgusted, could paint a good thing with a bad image very easily. Controversy was the easiest thing to generate. She cast a glance beside the door and there were a chain of small windows dangling in beautiful geometric shapes on the wall. She slid aside the lace drapes and peered in.

In the centre of the room there was a circular platform, covered with decorative Persian carpets and a large classical chandelier dropping down from the ceiling, similar to that in the palace, only this one had deep azure crystals instead of the white ones. It was a dazzling spotlight, radiating bronze, green and turquoise twinkles into the room. Girls barely dressed in clothes, which were obviously not meant to be used as clothes, were idly scattered around the platform quietly chatting to one another in the shadows. There were no males present, apart from a few black eunuchs in the right had corner of the room fingering their musical instruments. At the back of the room was a luxurious throne, snowed with silky purple and green cushions. Matching drapes hung over the privileged position.

That seat was obviously for Sheikh Khalil. Sara filtered through the myriad of girls seated in the shadows to see if Lulu was there in between them. Her eyes scanned the backless, strapless, sleeveless and neckless underwear type attire the girls were wearing. The curves of their navels, the crevasses of their breasts and the faint lines of their hips were all visible through the opaque fabric that they wore. To top off the oddness of the fashion, they were also adorned with jewels – they looked like demon fairies. Hopefully, Lulu would not be one of them.

Sara felt her fear turn into anger.

The demon fairies had an odd appearance. Not one had a drop of innocence apparent in their faces nor the white light that sparkles from ones face with immaturity. Here they all had plumped lips, lush cheeks and eyes intensified with kohl powder so as to appear the largest intoxicating feature on their sculpted faces. They threw out their shame and invited a complex by artificially emphasising the features on their face. In a way, Sara pitied them. It was a really hard task to be able to be content with only what one had, and not desire what they didn't. The only thing that Sara really wanted was her family back.

Sara scoured the mystical masks hidden in the shadows. Her eyes fell upon a girl sitting silently, in the darkest corner of the room. She was also adorned with gold jewels, armbands, a long necklace that fell between her breasts, bangles and a delicate chain which pronounced the undulating beauty of her curves. Her long eyelids hooded over her eyes, accentuated with kohl and glitter, which only revealed the deep glint of blue in her eyes further. The ebony hair fell in long wavy curls on her olive coloured shoulders She resembled a Golden Goddess secluded from the other colourful butterflies in the room.

It was Lulu.

Before Sara could recover from the shock, the music started playing and the careless whispers hushed down as a tall man
entered. He was garbed in saffron silk braided with gold, coupled with a white headscarf to match the ensemble of authority.
Mouth full lipped and a faint beard (presumably to hide the wrinkles) set in a broad shinning face, he sat down on the luxurious
throne. Two fanning girls kept him cool. He motioned to one of
the seated girls to stand on the circular platform. The manner in
which he did was as if he was selecting them from a basket of fruit.
'Begin,' he said. He sucked on his shisha and his image blurred as
a pillar of smoke rose around him. Now the picture was becoming
very clear.

Sheikh Khalil did not look like what Sara expected. His
son did not resemble him in the least. The only thing that was
similar was his build and the texture of the hair on his head. He
was slightly pop-eyed and his beard had a dry brush sort of texture.
A bevy of black slaves jabbed at him with trays of refreshments
and perfumes. Sara noticed that both his hands were heavily orna-
mented with rings. How disgustingly transsexual.

Drum and tale beats, deliberated rhythmically to represent
a melodious melt of physical sensations that set a trance around
the room. Even the carpets, rugs and numerous mirrors were affected by the masses of quaking bodies in the room. The voluptuous dancing girl's hips twisted and turned provocatively whilst the
girl on the central platform performed quite a different routine. It
was if she knew that she had to make new moves – gyrating and
gliding to set her apart from the other languid lasses present. One
could feel the fountains of love juice seeping onto their clothes,
affixing a thin wet film against their flesh.

Sara's eyes were immediately drawn to the contortions of their stomachs, and the way their muscles lapped at the air around them. Their skins broke into ripples all over their shiny bodies. They shook and slithered like tiny demons performing a dance of exorcism around a fire. The fire here, was the elderly Sheikh.

Crystals reflected light in miniature patterns on alcoves in the ceiling. Carefully restored purple, green and blue mosaics garnished the walls. One could never imagine that this tower was embedded in the centre of a sun-blanched mud field, behind sweeping sand dunes surrounded with pocketfuls of dust.

The feeling was queer. Shamelessly salacious and vulgar. An eroticised, exoticised exhibition of mesmerised maidens who actually wanted to be a decoration piece of the room.

Sara felt sick. A ball of vomit rolled inside of her.

She turned away and crouched on the floor. Her back faced the door. Everything felt incredibly moist. She found that she was sweating at the rate of a rainstorm. It must be true then, she recalled. A male cannibal! No wonder Atif remains detached from the unbridled hedonism his father chooses to indulge in.

She closed her hot eyes.

But was Atif really better? Did he want to capture these voyeuristic fantasies and make dolls out of them? As the blister of reality popped, Sara's head started spinning. Ten years she had spent of her life entrapping the explicit apparel that this father and son clothe themselves with: the Father dwelling in physicality, the Son devouring the mentality.

For a moment she had forgotten about Lulu, but was reminded by Mimmy's sudden appearance.

'Arwa, what are you doing?' Mimmy said. She panted towards her sister like a rupture in the madness that surrounded them. 'Did you find Lulu?'

There was no reply. Just sandy rivulets cascading down a cracked face split in two.

Having to witness her sister torn apart like this was not unexpected. Mimmy crouched down beside her sister and took her hand.

'Arwa, Lulu is safe,' she said, but quickly stopped. There was no getting through to her sister. 'Come on, let's go to our room. Lulu will be back in the morning,'

Sara stood up, encapsulated in her stupor. They walked slowly. Silence lodged itself obstinately between them.

They tried to sleep, but only one of them did.

The door thud quite loudly. There stood Lulu, the Golden Goddess. Her head sagged down the middle of her chest. She was crying with such force that Sara could even see a river of emotion spilling onto her cheeks.

'Oh Arwa!. You would never believe what I have been through! They will kill me. I escaped. I shouldn't have done that, but I did.'

Nervousness clawed the flesh on Sara's back, in short penetrative movements.

'I decorated the room in the morning with flowers and perfume oils,' Lulu said. 'We lit the perfume and it made the air thick with a winding essence. I don't know what occurred in me – but I wanted to find out what happened in the night time.' She gulped. 'I went to put the baskets away and found that in the room next door. Rawia was leading young girls which had arrived from a carriage outside. It was obvious that they were the maidens who visited the harem at night. They wore costumes laid out on the bed from which each chose one. I was careful not to let Rawia see me and I went into the room. None of the girls seemed to know one another so no one spoke to me either. On the bed was a golden outfit, with matching jewels in a chest beside the bed. I dressed up in it.'

The same part of her mind which rebuked her when Andrew took her for a ride scolded her. 'Why did you do that Lulu, why?' Sara asked, not wanting to hear what happened, but at the same time anxious about what did.

'I don't know. I guess I wanted the romance, the adventure, something exciting to happen to me,' she whispered. 'We were told by a black eunuch what we had to do. It seemed relatively easy. 'Just dance when the music starts and if you are called onto the platform, you are the jewel of the night' he said. I was excited. The music played and I could feel the rhythm in my head. It did not occur to me at the time that this was not a ladies-only affair. It was wonderful. Then the problem started. The girl on the platform did not please the Sheikh so he pointed to me. I felt phobiatic, I have never danced in my life. In our tribes the men dance and the women watch.'

Their voices woke up Mimmy. She slid over to where both were seated on the floor. 'Lulu, how was it?' she asked. Her eyes twinkled with envy and excitement, but the others did not notice this reaction.

'Disgusting! I don't know what happened. We were all playing a game, the elements of which everyone was aware of, but me. I tried to move like the girl before me but I couldn't. I could feel the Sheikh's eyes watching, gnawing every piece of my flesh. He devoured my innocence, my inability to please. I felt as if I was a painting, being hung on a wall for people to stare at every brushstroke. Then he called me into the room at the top of the tower. I didn't want to go, but I realised that I had to or I could be stoned. In the room it was just me and him. He came barricading towards me, parading in passion. Satan strives in these situations. I knew I felt him around me, in the room with us, whispering evil things to the Sheikh. I fell onto the circular bed, and tried to hide behind the veils. But he could see me. He was offering me some milk and honey but somehow it dripped on my navel. He bent to lick it off. Before his lips could touch me I screamed. He was drunk and his eyes looked as if they were climbing, step by step into a memory. I doubt he is even Muslim. I managed to unlock the door and escape from there, but I could hear the eunuchs behind me. Black ones, white ones all of them. When I turned, they blended into a grey army. I must hide this dress. They don't know I am a worker in the palace.' She stripped off the dress and jewels, stuffing them into the materials baskets. Then she slipped into bed beside Sara, clutching her in fright. They all slept.

'Allah Hu Akbar, Allah Hu Akbar.'

Sara's puffed eyelids raised themselves to pray. She turned her face to see whether Lulu was awake. Lulu was not in the room. She *never* missed Fajr. Both Mimmy and Sara were terrified.

Lulu was found spiritless, unable to face her Lord, dead out of debauchery in the courtyard. The Ghost of Ecstasy had cursed her.

Chapter 13

The previous night was not a peaceful one. His father had returned early from the harem, drunk and swamped in a stinking rage. A gradual dread bustled up inside Atif as he heard his father stomping towards his room, kneading the marble floor with each footprint. He rose to his feet before Khalil battered the door down.

'Atif, Atif I want to talk to you,' he bellowed in between belches. A faint buzzing sound moved around with him.

'Yes Abati[1]?' he answered dryly.

His father was an epitomy of cursedness. Khalil staggered in, barely making a step at a time, foolishly losing the respect, the dignity that use to spread like a glow into the room years ago. Atif struck his eyes away from Khalil's appearance, so as not to be affected by his delirious state.

'Atif, you are thirty five years old and you have still not produced an heir to manage our assets?'

His son was busy staring at his mother's portrait on the wall. From her position on the wall, she gave him comfort.

'Why don't you come to the harem and take your pick out of one of my girls? Atif, I am talking to you.'

'Abati, you know that I do not agree with your lavish activities, we are Muslim, all of this is forbidden.' The rest of the sentence stuck in his throat. It was a waste trying to get Abati to understand, he never would, as much as he wanted him to return to being the father he always knew. Detached from an early age from his mother, who had become mad, his father had brought him up. Then, after a long business trip to Turkey he began his drinking, the obsession of keeping a chamber of women arose and he even stopped praying. The European influence seeped into him like a toxic addition at an unsustainable rate. Khalil was saturated to the brim of his skin membranes with a chemical that was evidently shortening his life.

'You must produce an heir soon Atif. I am warning you!'

'I am surprised you haven't produced one for me yet, Abati.'

Khalil ignored him. 'There was this girl there today, she was as fragile as a golden butterfly and as innocent as a young sapling. If you want we can hunt her down and you can marry her. I am convinced she will produce a beautiful heir for you. Take fruit of the mastic tree with oil and honey, it will keep you unharmed in the darkest of nights. It's a lovely potion, a tried and tested love device. Want some wine?' he asked.

'Abati, I think you should go and rest, I have yet to see a woman who is respectable and loyal. A woman who will only want to please me and not the other men who stare at her. Abati, you possess a lingering shadow which follows you everywhere. Not many can see it, but I have always seen it trailing behind you, like a tail.'

Khalil put his goblet down. 'Great, the wonderful shadow theory again. Where do you come up with these things? I must speak to the ministers to educate you on logic. My dear son, don't you know that everything in this universe has a shadowy side? Allah has created us that way.' His tone was sharp, trying his best to avert the assertion that he knew would follow. 'The only thing that does not have a shadow is the sun. If you take things so literally, the next thing you'll be claiming is that the only truthfulness in this world is the sun!' he said.

A crisp chill stood between them. Before it could intervene in the exchange, Khalil left, defeated as usual but not wounded.

The evening was unusually dry. The shaft of the golden afternoon sun shrank slim, but left an unpleasant crackle in the air. One could feel their skin shrink with lack of moisture beneath their clothes. Even the usually soft pads of skin on the soles of Atif's pedicured feet were wrung out of their wetness. His nose felt vacuumed right from the tip to the crown of his head: a hasty lobotomy. It was a prickly heat, stinging the back of his throat with its ferociously primitive kisses.

Atif plopped into his cushions, and tried to get comfortable. He liked to spend his mornings, his evenings, and his nights alone in solitude. Beside him to the left lay stacks of sweet smelling frankincense which he had to approve for quality. On his right, was a pot full of furry coffee beans, fresh, mahogany and powdery. Their family monopolised the incense trade and the coffee trade and yet, at the prime of his manhood he had no heir to continue the enterprise.

He looked up at the portrait of his mother. A familiar terror gripped him by the throat as he recalled tormenting memories of his mother. For years, and years he had to live believing that his father was innocent, forced to turn his back to reality, otherwise his father would murder him too. The worst part was that he could not discuss it with anyone. If he did he would lose both parents. Then he would be totally abandoned, isolated in a palace with people who were there just for the sake of being there. If he wanted to be heard, he had to shout. But no one that cared would listen. He didn't expect an audience like Abati, but he expected compassion. He wondered where it was hidden.

A cloud crackled in the distance. Its cheeks blew enormous until it finally coughed out sprinkles of rain on the bands of sand, eroding the floor into a pattern of sieves. Pools of tears here and there shone like polished silver. But the shadowless entity, the burning sun, soon sucked the palate dry. An instant summer storm.

There was a thump on the door. Not a muffled knock like his servants, but an angry, loud, battering one. A red faced girl marched in, the glitter in her eyes peeping through a curly busk of hair that lifted up into an untamed puff at the top of her head.

Atif stood up, startled at the sight before him.

Sara gritted her teeth, unable to decide what to say. The harder she clamped them, the more her tears squirted out. Lulu was her friend, her companion, together they mothered Mimmy. Now Lulu was gone. Bartered to the other world. Simply because of Khalil. Lulu couldn't face her Lord, the Lord she loved, the one whom she never compromised her meeting before dawn with. And now, because of Khalil, Lulu for the first time was ashamed. Her blood splattered around her in gel-like puddles on the courtyard which she slammed down upon.

He waited for the steaming, silent girl to say something. He didn't know her to be of the servant girls of the palace, so *who* was she?

'Lulu is dead,' she managed to whisper between breaths.

'Lulu?'

'Yes Lulu.' She burst into a fountain of tears.

They stood there like two shrubs embedded in desert sand dunes, chilled by the nightly gales: one hot, quaking, repulsive, the other frozen by the ignition sent out by the first.

The clear glass crystals of the chandelier chimed above them.

'Sit down, and tell me what happened.' His mysterious gaze

was calculated to ooze right into her.

She was stifled. Rattling like a tambourine, she obeyed. She didn't know how to begin. If she started cursing Khalil's amorous arousals she would risk both Mimmy and her own future at the palace. They could be beheaded. She might have lost family, but she could not afford to lose yet another home.

Atif poured some mint tea for Sara. As he bent down to offer it to her some he smelt the swooning scents that had entombed themselves in Sara's hair from the night before. He was lost in the midst of her dark, shiny curls drawing him in deeper and deeper with their cotton softness.

'You told us to make dolls,' Sara said 'But I saw what kind of women you wanted us to make miniatures of. It was so you could keep records of how many you have used.' Immediately after she had said it, she wished that she hadn't.

She must have seen the harem, poor girl, deduced Atif, suddenly recognising who she was. 'My father has his leisure at the expense of young women-,' he gulped. 'These women are not forced into doing what they do, they do it out of their own lustful desires. For years I have watched him adorn them with jewels in return for a night of pleasure.' He watched Sara's eyes growing wider and wider as the alibi thickened. 'I never agreed with it, when you arrived with your little sister and friend was when he began abusing the harem. You needed a job and I felt that if we kept a record, one day he would realise how disgraceful his character has become.'

'And has that day come?'

'No.'

'My friend Lulu lost her life because of your father, she was a part of my family!' She repeated the daunting fact, the words barely left her lips. 'She killed herself in the courtyard this morning because she could not face her Lord with what she had done.' The sour taste slid back into her mouth. Her eyes welled up again.

'You are not the only one who has lost family!' He found his victim, he needed a victim, after all these years he finally found one. He pounced on the opportunity like a beggar.

'Arwa,' he said, 'what I am about to tell you has remained only between myself and Allah. No one is aware of what I have witnessed.' He paused, as if trying to slow down the rate of the words, feelings, emotions swelling in his mouth. 'We used to be a happy family, myself, my mother and I. My parents were deep in affection for one another and they loved me dearly. Then, when I was eight years old. I heard my mother who was pregnant roar with pain in the night from somewhere in the palace. Hastily, I went to see where she was, she had given birth or was giving birth – I never managed to find out. I saw my father leave with a small bundle in his hands, cautiously as if not to be seen by the servants or maids. My mother kept screaming, yelling, I crouched outside the door unable to understand any of this. Her screams still pierce my ear drums today.' Tears crept down his troubled face, knowing that they had to be released. He continued, turning towards the blurry portrait of his mother.

'I followed Abati, but he disappeared so quickly I did not know what he was doing or where he was going. I stood by the window pane, shivering in horror. That's when I heard it. A cry, a baby's cry quickly muffled by a sharp thud. I looked out of the window and saw Abati bury a baby in the secluded corner of the courtyard. I watched fistfuls of dry, cracked mud being hurled at my bother or sister, as it tried to wriggle in its tiny little grave. Then I fainted. Next morning, my mother, Noha, went mad. She was crying for 'her baby princess,' agonising, scratching on the walls, every day her condition got worse. And every day my father yelled at the Hakim until one day, the madness never escaped into the palace again. My mother died.'

Sara got up. She was taken aback by the terror in this man's life. 'But why, why did you not tell anyone about your sister?'

'Because if I did, Abati would kill me too. And I know he killed Ummi[2] and that means he would definitely kill me too. But I loved him, and he loved me too. He used to spend more and more time with me after Ummi died. After a while I forgot he was a murderer!'

A cool, gentle spring of relief flowed upon him. The load was shed, it was separate from him, sitting at his feet. He was freed. Released from his hammering silence. She watched wordlessly at how this smart, respectable character was actually so vulnerable as melted wax. The reason for his eerie silence was buried, locked and clasped shut in his forfeited childhood. His back was still towards her, hunched towards the large illustration on the wall, hiccupping in tears of grief.

Although she felt important to have found that she was worthy of such information, Sara was confused. She felt her heart climb down. Invisible rain wrinkled up the streaks of her annoyance into nothing. She wanted to walk up to Sheikh Atif and hug the unswerving pain pellets out of him, but she knew she couldn't.

Atif shook his head back, and stood upright. He longed for a touch, a mortal touch to powder the spiky nerves which invaded every corner of his body. He turned towards Sara. Their eyes did the talking for them. She stood, embalmed in emotion, curdling with desire. He stepped towards her, wanting to smother her in hot caresses.

His deep, silent confidence infuriated her. His slight smile and lowered stares made things move inside of her, sending bubbling reactions everywhere. Nothing made sense. The entrapment was the green glare that penetrated out of his eyes, capturing her eyes into their force. It was a glorious feeling of elation.

'I think I should leave now,' she said. She rushed away leaving a waft of jasmine in the air, darting out of his garrulous gaze in an instant.

[1] 'My father,' in Arabic

Chapter 14

Mimmy observed her reflection in the mirror as she brushed her hair back into two parts. She had changed over the years, spurted into a unique butterfly. The only problem was, she wasn't allowed to roam freely amongst nature. She even carried the symbol of experience proudly on her shoulders, that slight forward hunch of the tip of the shoulders which married women had from years of embracing their husbands. Mimmy evolved into that shape naturally, without ever having to embrace any man. Lulu had had her taste and fulfilment and she was not strong enough to handle it. Poor Lulu. But *she* was. Mimmy knew what she wanted, and she knew she could handle it.

The sisters spent the morning washing Lulu's spiritless body. It was limp, floppy, and exempt from the presence which gave it any meaning. Lulu's vessel was sterilised and ready for the burial. They lay her on white cotton, metres and metres of it, parcelling her up like the womb sac she once burst out of.

Mimmy folded up the clothes. Their simplicity bothered her. Lulu had been special. She fingered the stitching on the hem, her feelings returning to Lulu. It was very generous of Sheikh Atif to offer to have such a grand funeral for Lulu, she thought. People normally forgot about their servants.

It wasn't that she did not miss Lulu. It was just that she couldn't understand why she would have ended her life after a night of a lifetime. Her sister entered, the pain of the loss carved into her face like a monument. For a moment, the sight of Lulu's

147

desolate bed reawakened both their sorrows. Soon a eunuch boy knocked on the door, reminding them that they had to be present for the reading of the Qur'an and the funeral prayer. They rushed down-stairs, wrapping themselves appropriately with their veils.

They made their way to the mosque for the Janazah prayer. The female section was buzzing with maids, servants and other ladies that Sara had never seen. It was a relief to see so many people ready to offer their condolences for Lulu. Although she was a recent convert, watching Lulu pray repeatedly had acquainted them quite closely with the faith. There was no way to evoke or practice Judaism: no siddur, no synagogue, no family, no Jew. So when they had to turn to God, they turned to Allah. After all, he was the same God, it was the way a person showed Him gratitude that was different.

Mimmy perched herself in a corner and picked up a volume of the Qur'an. She didn't like the sound and tone of the passage, it was far too harsh and domineering. She turned a few pages. The words capered triumphantly on the page, digging themselves into her. Mimmy clamped the holy book shut.

Rawia was seated beside her, noticing her terror. Religion does not enlighten those who do not seek it, she thought. She handed her a tasbeeh[1] to recite 'Allah Hu Akbar,' a hundred times, using each bead. That was easy. In their Arabic lessons Mimmy had learnt these practices off by heart

The situation that Sara was experiencing was quite different. The Qur'an was arranged in two piles – the right pile consisted of volumes which had been read, the left pile which needed to be read; the former shorter than the latter. She took the top volume on the left pile and clutched it to her chest, walking amidst the white hills of ladies reciting verses to themselves on the floor. They arrived blank and they left blank. The white spoke the reality of it all.

The room resembled an identity of what the palace tried to hide; sterile, morbid and lifeless. The blankness accentuated the void in Sara's life. She crouched near the door, between two of the plump cooks, sheltering herself from the bitterness which cleaved to her like the closeness of the relationship between the water barrier and a foetus. Sara prayed, Why God, do I lose everyone that I love? Aren't I permitted any love in my destiny? Oh Allah, I may not be a devout Muslim but accept my prayer. Please keep Mother, Lulu and Daud safe and worthy of heaven for surely, You know the best.

A fragment of her soul and a spiritual tear fell on the leather cover of the Qur'an, and dribbled its way across to the spine as Sara opened the book. Her own parents never troubled to teach her how to read Hebrew, and there she was, reading the Qur'an in fluent Arabic. She carried on a bit further. The verses made things move inside of her. The words blew sympathy onto her wounds.

It was clear to her now. She was dropped in this situation to find closeness to God. This was her test. She was born for this. She had the perfect environment and everything she needed to find meaning in her life to establish a vital level of understanding which was missing. The only distinction was that it was a different faith to what her mother had taught her. There was no point in continuing being something when she *knew* nothing about it and could *do* nothing of it and *practice* nothing for it. As she proceeded through the passage, she felt herself drawn in towards this newfound faith, this clear cut way of life. A wisp of spirituality finally awakened inside of her, the light spreading to the tip of her toes.

Sara decided that she was going to re-convert and start a new life: refresh and renew her transformation for good.

Later that evening, Sara practiced the conversation she would have with Rawia. She decided to subtly ask Rawia for guidance in the matter. Of course, she would not let it be known that it was for herself that she was asking, for Rawia had always believed that they were Muslims.

She found Rawia sewing sequins onto what looked like an aubergine bed spread. Bolster cushions and ribbons were scattered around her like ruffles snipped off a rainbow. She was even more lost in the folds than was the needle that dived through the fabric.

Sara tapped on the door gently. Rawia didn't stir. She tapped a bit harder, using her nails to grasp her attention. This time Rawia looked up.

'Finally,' Sara said. She had begun to sweat nervously, the moisture seeping onto the tight fabric under her arms.

'Assalamoalaikum.'

'Walaikum assalam.'

'What are you sewing?'

'It's a bedspread,'

'Another one?' It was very strange that Rawia always sewed bedspreads, and it was always for the same room: Sheikh Atif's bedroom. His feminine taste struck her once again as she examined the delicate velvet appliqué on the border of a bolster cushion.

Rawia nodded, casting a pleased look at the handiwork that was engulfing most of the room like a high tide.

'Rawia, I need your help. You know that I am not as well

read in religion as you are, and I was hoping you could guide me in the basics for someone to convert to Islam.' The words toppled over one another in a single breath.

Rawia raised a thin eyebrow. She was clearly surprised at the suggestion, although Sara felt that she had no reason to be so. 'Arwa,' she said, putting her sewing down, 'everyone here is a Muslim. Who are you acquainted with who does not know the basics?'

Sara blushed. 'I am just inquiring as a point of knowledge, in case someone came to me for advice. I would not know how to begin.' She wished Rawia's eyes were not so focused on her, she felt that the sharp rays they emitted were interrogating her. To her surprise, Rawia got up and wrote a few things on a piece of paper. The quill glided with ease against the paper. It was a relief to see it dance so quickly to Rawia's command.

'Here you go,' she said. She put the small scroll into Sara's lap. 'I hope you find it useful.'

'Shukran! Shukran' Sara said, but then realised she must not overreact. She floated out of the room, excitement simmering inside of her. She wanted to share her new found spirituality with Mimmy.

Mimmy was absent.

She picked up a saintly candle to light the thicker, shorter ones. She lit every single candle, even bringing out extras to place on the floor. It was a special day today. The room glowed with golden candle light, casting projections of the cutwork of the bronze lanterns on all four white walls. A golden spirit swam on the ceiling. A soul rolled out of the floor and clung to the depths of her empty body. After making the required ablutions, she perched herself on the edge of the bed and revealed the contents of the scroll. She knew that she had to sincerely believe in and then recite the declaration of her faith:

'La ilaha illallah Muhammad ur Rasul Allah'
'There is no God but Allah, Muhammad is Allah's messenger.'

Although she didn't know much about the Prophet Muhammad (peace be upon him), she knew she believed in him. Not because she just wanted to convert. Not because she wanted to feel closer to Lulu. But because she had surrendered herself to destiny. She had a set place in this world and she could, for once, yield herself spiritually as well as physically. He held authority after Allah and his book. She unrolled the curling ends of the crisp scroll. It was covered with elegant Arabic calligraphy:

1.Basic Beliefs:
Tawhid – oneness of Allah
Risalah – prophets
Akhirah – life after death

2.The main source of Law in Islam is the Qur'an, which was sent down to the Prophet through the angel Jibrail. Hadith are sayings of the Prophet which aid in keeping with the Islamic way of life.

3.Duties as a Muslim:
Shahadah – declaration of faith
Salah – five compulsory daily prayers
Zakat – welfare contribution
Hajj – pilgrimage to Mecca
Sawm – fasting in Ramadan.

She cast her eyes through it once again. The basic beliefs she knew she could locate from the Qur'an, she knew most of them anyway, living amongst Arabs all her life. She would have to find out what the the duties were from Rawia or even Sheikh Atif, if he would let her. After all, he had related a deep secret to her the other day. She felt he could return her the favour. She lay her head back on the pillow. Tonight the blank white room was strong enough to inspire dreams in colour. Now calm and at ease, she fell asleep.

The door creaked open. Mimmy stepped in quietly, surprised at the warm bright light that sparkled in the room. She crept about, blowing each candle out, one by one, until there was only one left, above Arwa.

As if telepathically sensing Mimmy's presence in the depth of her slumber, Sara awoke. 'Mimmy! You're back! I can't wait to share with you what I have found today!'

Mimmy stood coldly in front of her. 'I have something to share with you too Arwa.'

'Well, shall I go first?' Sara said.

'No, I think I had better.'

'Fine go ahead,' Sara said, beaming at her from her position on the bed.

'We all have choices to make my sister, and I have made mine after due consideration.' Mimmy looked out the window. 'I want to be renowned, admired, cherished for what I can be – I do not want to spend the rest of my life sewing stupid dolls.' She looked back Sara. 'I can't keep making dolls any more,' she blurted out, 'I want to become one.'

'Become one what?'

Mimmy looked back out of the window.

There was no other way to say it more clearly.

Mimmy's words barked into Sara's ears, biting them off with their ferociousness. Her heart pulled on the line. This was her sister, the sister, whom she had served so hard to create a respectable life for. Snapping all the threads she had built her cradle with, she wanted to become one of the prostitutes!

'What, a Prostitute!?' A rising of blood choked her breath, as she tried to understand what Mimmy was telling her. She managed to stand up, fury curdling viciously inside of her. 'You *want* to be a prostitute? You *want* to be looked upon as some object of desire? How could you do this?' she yelled, clenching her teeth to prevent all the sanity escaping from her mouth.

'I will be liberated.'

'LIBERATED! The only thing you are liberating Mimmy is male promiscuity!' she screamed.

'You can come with me too.'

'You are *not* going.'

Mimmy repeated the offer ignoring the decision that her sister had made for her. 'You can come with me too.'

'YOU ARE NOT GOING! I will only wish you death so you will commit less sins.'

'If you remain fixated on death you will only weep, Arwa. Recall the attributes of mercy instead, and you will feel better,' Mimmy said.

'Whatever you do, don't die a hypocrite,' Sara said. 'They bear the lowest level of all. Relying on mercy is the sign of hypocrites! Why should God listen to you when you never tried to understand him?' She slapped and clawed Mimmy, who fell to the floor with fright at the beating. Sara continued thrashing her, when suddenly the black purdah tore apart.

Inside was a scarlet outfit, resembling that of the girls in the forbidden chamber. Sara stared in horror at the flesh which gaped at her from the stripped clothing her sister was wearing.

'You...you have already been to this place? You have already been *penetrated?*' She looked away. Here she was, going to share her spirituality with her sister, the person she loved the most dearly in the world, who she had hoped would share the same passion. But she had already chosen her path that lead straight to an abyss in Hell.

Mimmy stumbled up, towering over her sister's hunched body, which spilled itself all over the room.

'You don't have to do this Mimmy. You know it is wrong!'

Mimmy gathered some of her belongings into a bundle. Nothing made a difference. 'You want to come with me Arwa? We could have an exotic life together, we could be a duet. You don't know what you are missing.'

The silence slapped her sharply in the face.

Then she left.

The fading candle tried hard to save its last breath.

The wick bent its head, anticipating a curse.

And the last candle blew out, all by itself.

Sara became Arwa once and for all.

Chapter 15

Content with his appearance for the ceremony, Sergeant Murad departed from the training grounds in his crisp military uniform. The red turban on his head symbolised his hard work and achievement, and the sloped black thobe1 in itself pronounced his authority. He marched out, amongst the numerous white soldiers who were also to receive commendation. As each one passed the exit on horseback they shot a final glance at the crumbly rocky outcrops that they had mastered their skills upon. The steep cones and sharp ridges that they climbed were terrifyingly hazardous, making their victory all the more sweet.

Murad stared up towards one of the caves where he had spent days as Team Leader reassuring his team mates that they would survive the task. In the dark cramped space they had spent a fortnight with minimal allowances of food. They were forced to survive on the dispensed shrubs which occasionally sprouted in shaded areas. Unfortunately, two other teams had lost a member each, in the suffering conditions and were mummified the very next day. One of the men had been Murad's partner in canon firing. It was a big shock to him as they embalmed him in locally found gum and wrapped him in linen from flax which Sheikh Atif had especially imported from Egypt for the military cadets. This gesture was considered supportive of the soldier's hard work, but it was disturbing to them since the Sheikh deliberately had funeral preparations ready in case they were needed. It was a curt reminder of the tyrannical training and the rigorous discipline it tamed their personal desires with.

Spears flung into the air, drilling holes into the sky as they pivoted to their target. Shields clanged in mock duels. Their moves were adept, their experience was mastered and their responses quickened. The essence of a powerful army was captured in each one of these soldiers. Under the low, blinding sun they qualified and were now to receive distinctions.

An itch bit into Murad's hope.

Load shedding was not a part of his nature. As a child he was trained into looking at the brighter side of things. After all, his parents had sold him, hadn't they? For all they knew, Murad could have been used for bad jobs. Camel racing being one of them. Those poor, isolated toddlers, sold by their parents in exchange for empty promises of better futures to rich, greedy sheikhs who used them as jockeys for gambling. The lighter the child, the better the camel performed. Barely fed, these children were forced to ride camels at the expense of their skin splitting and their bones visibly hanging out. His partner in the army had had his child snatched from him for camel racing.

His camel balked, and he was forced to let the animal rest.

Once, Murad had left the palace in search of a better life, which a gardener had talked him into. He had acquainted himself with a devious sheikh who wanted him to kidnap little boys and girls below the age of five for a tremendous price. The sheikh said that he would train them and educate them, away from the poverty-ridden holes they dwelled in. Murad kidnapped a child, sincerely believing that he was doing the best for the baby. However, on the way back to the sheikh's dwelling he felt a rugged sack suffocating him, forcing his blood to vibrate. Then he fled for his life, back to the palace, dropping the scummy baby back to its poverty hole. The world was as corrupt as a thief, and as conclusive as a corpse. Since then, he sincerely repented everyday, begging the Lord to grant him his peace back.

And one day his peace invited itself back. He felt the rumblings of delight banter within his usually dull casing. Allah was kind. Allah was always kind. A blurred image skimmed in his imagination, it was seen so often in his dreams that it evolved into a close reality that he could touch, feel, sense. This sensation is called one-sided attraction. Unlike the old Sheikh who monopolised the hearts of women with his words, wealth and wit, Murad liked to wait. Such an outlook was brought about by his principles. Accomplishment of aims within the prescribed limits was the final level, and he accepted the challenge.

The camel smiled at him, bringing an essence of life into the sound of the lonely desert wind. Murad remounted, trying his best to catch up with the hoof beats further ahead of him.

Something else pinched him.

One night as he was grieving the loss of his partner, he had made for the rocky outcrops to disperse the negative energy out of his system. Higher and higher, rock after rock, he managed to reach a significant height. Threads of sweat salinised his nutty skin. He rested upon two rocks tilted against one another. He threw his aching head back, his body sprawled upwards and face the stars. As he did so, a rock fell out of the arrangement piled up behind him. The stone crackled and rubbed past others on its way down to Earth. He jumped. A strong, rotten stench, almost human followed. Initially his reaction was that of terror, in case he had intruded into an animal's cave. But then, a silver hook shaped twinkle caught his eye. The intensity of the flashes brightened with the appearance of the full moon. He approached the hole cautiously, the decaying stench numbed his head, he clamped his nostrils shut. He hauled away the giant boulders to see what was inside.

It was a pile of men, three to be exact. They were dressed in fraying royal outfits; cream thobes and black robes. Their faces possessed that eroded, eaten-away look which people who were victims to lethal diseases had. The insect kingdom drilled a dungeon of holes into the meat, munching and crunching their way through the rotting flesh. Who could they be? As far as he knew Sheikh Khalil and Sheikh Atif were the only royals around. Syedati Noha had died many years ago, and no one was aware of any other relatives. Extremely mysterious.

A hot bead of sweat trickled down his forehead and down the slope of his nose, until it finally attached itself to the edge of his right nostril. Had he made a discovery lethal to his future? He had somehow made his way back to the tent, the drooped expressions on the dead faces swooning in front of him with each step. What could he do? He could not tell either of the Sheikhs, they would dismiss him from the army if it was an internal scandal. Yet his conscience gambled with him, robbing him of a peaceful night's sleep that night of long ago.

They approached the palace entrance. The hoots of birds bounded against the sharp angles of the rocks. His back stiffened.

'Men! Dismount and march into the hall!' the Sergeant Major barked.

The two hundred men obeyed and marched erect behind Murad into the hall. The hall was appropriately decorated, covered in banners of the red, green, blue and white stripes that dictated levels of achievement, and ribbons hung vertically from the enormous chandeliers. The men stood in parallel lines, whilst the senior officers sat opposite them in over-sized maroon velvet chairs. Though the velvet chairs were meant to brand the sitter with authority, Murad felt that it was more of a punishment to sit on a hot, clammy seat in the middle of the beastly desert. Placed amongst the senior officers, Murad didn't feel so superior anymore. His red turban and sash were incomparable to the green, blue and white ones that gaped to his left. *Alhumdulillah, I should be grateful that I have made it this far.* He would earn that white turban one day InshAllah, and make sure he'd deserve it. He pushed away the stifling presence of the senior officers which belittled him.

The lutes twanged to the feverish rhythms of the drums and the procession opened with a jambiya dance by some of the cadets. The audience clapped to the beats as the circles of men swayed their daggers and sticks in the air in a synchronised manner. Others wiggled their bottoms, an unusual task for men. The average man has firm rounded cheeks, but the Arab has tremendous control over all his muscles. Many clues about race and culture were evident by just watching a snippet of the vigorous dance. In their white outfits the men resembled hens pecking and clucking monotonously for the rooster, until eventually their urge would be satisfied.

The tempo slowed down, and Sheikh Atif entered, accompanied with two assistants. He stepped up gallantly onto the stage, with the elegance of a dove and the confidence of a falcon yoked into one. 'Assalamoalaikum brothers,' his strong, sturdy voice bounced in a straight line to the back wall.

'Walaikum assalam rehmatullahi-wabara kahtahu,' the army chimed.

'I would like to begin with congratulating each and every one of you in reaching this far. You, yourselves have been acquainted with a discipline and honour that is incomparable to any other occupation in this country. Your promise to serve against the personal up-surging aspirations you may have will always be commended with honour and dignity ....'

The speech resumed for quite a while, whilst Murad focused on the shiny reflection of himself in his brown leather shoes. He knew that he should have been listening attentively, but in his heart, the distinguished praise of all of his achievements were to Allah, for making it all possible. It was time for the awards only when the General went forward to receive his jambiya sword. The crowds hooted with admiration. A babble of noise rose upwards to the stage following each presentation. When his name was called, Murad stood up slowly. If only he had a mother or a father to witness this achievement.

Atif smiled and congratulated Sergeant Murad Mohammed with a silver jambiya. Murad accepted it with military skill and swayed it to his side in one elegant gesture.

'I hope to see you higher up in the ranks soon,' whispered Atif impressed with the overflowing vitality and strength that seeped into the hall with the presence of the young man.

'InshAllah,' replied Murad. He stared into the crystal green eyes in pleasure. When he resumed his position, his cheeks were painted with tints of praise.

A few more stripes of excellence were awarded to cadets, who tied them to their left arm as it was customarily done in the army, and then the ceremony finally closed. The men held a celebration of their own, performing a jambiya dance. It was a narrative that each person had learnt by heart, the clicking, the stamping and the pouncing at a certain, precise moment.

Murad removed his sweaty turban, heaving a deep sigh of relief. He wondered what Arwa, Mimmy and Lulu were doing. They were his only friends, his childhood playmates whom he could relate to. He untied the leather straps of his shoes. He

161

wanted to celebrate his achievement with gifts for all of them. So, he quickly changed into a fresh new futah[2] and headed for the nearest suq.

Quarters of silversmiths, leather workers, rug sellers and pottery stalls were the initial enticement of the suq. Further intrusion uncovered clutters of intricate goods, ranging from traditional hand woven wall hangings to large mint tea holders. An Egyptian man clutched Murad and thrust a bundle of qat under his nose. Murad shrugged him off, tripping over the rocky alleyway. A few girls, well curved and fair, stood eyeing him from a corner. They jangled their bangles to catch his attention. When he refused to respond, they shook their cowrie shell head dresses. Upon hearing the unusual sound of shells clacking together, Murad turned around and blushed. He quickly skipped out of their view, cutting from a small area between two coffee pot stalls.

The square bloated with smoke from a cheap, greasy restaurant. Minty aromas swerved madly above soft kebabs roasting on bonfires. One step to a trade in life, food, a step further and there lurks the trade in death. Second-hand swords, knives and arrows, standing on their points, waited to prick, shred and skin, were stacked in the space behind the kebab shack.

The smell of roasted pistachios and warm spiced cashews wafted between stalls in a nutty scent. As he drifted his way through the evening bustle, he came across many items that could be ideal. Cloths, fans, rings, Bedouin cuffs, beaded bags and shawls. Having never bought a female a present before, he had to think very carefully as to what would be suitable. For Mimmy it was easy, she loved talking about fashionable women, so a kohl box would surprise her.

Passing a few more scattered stalls, his eyes caught sight of a small comb. 'How much for the comb?' he asked. He rummaged in his pocket for some money. To his surprise, it didn't cost very much and he happily smiled to himself at the bargain. Lulu would sparkle as the delicate teeth floated through her silken hair. He slid it into his pocket pleased with the choices he had made. He was more content with the items themselves than the money spent.

Then it was the difficult present. Arwa was a simple girl, grateful and polite for anything that she would receive. But Murad wanted to give her something memorable, significant enough to remind her of his special instincts towards her.

In the corner of the market he saw a silversmith's jewellery stall, shooting darts of light on nearby stalls. The table was laden with rings, lockets, pendants, bangles and anklets. His eyes fell on a silver handcuff, engraved delicately and laid with a single red stone. She will love this, he thought to himself and excitedly asked the value. One day I will get you real rubies, Arwa.

'Six ducats,' the old silversmith replied.

'Six ducats?' he confirmed the price as he calculated that it was all he had remaining of his monthly salary. 'Is there any chance of you lowering the price?'

The man smiled. 'Son, everyday I work under considerable pressure to feed my family. Do you think that I am really asking for too much?'

'But surely the customer's don't taunt you.'

'No, the customers are friendly. But my peers know that I am the only Jew in this area and take advantage of that fact when they have nothing better to do. They are my friends, don't get me wrong. They would hold their lives at stake for me, but some people don't know when a joke has worn out.' He drew out a kippah, which he had scrunched away into his pocket so as to minimise attacks on his appearance.

Murad handed him the money without any bargaining. He

wanted to get something extra special for Arwa, and no price was too expensive for her. He was satisfied with his purchases but he wondered how they would react to his military uniform the following morning. He planned to wake up early to have plenty of time to iron his uniform to perfection.

The welcome was not what he expected.

On the way to his destination he was met with many strange glares which questioned his opting to clothe himself in uniform on a weekend. His uniform was impressively pressed with every crease as sharp as a blade. He knocked on the door.

Arwa opened it. She looked thin, drained and yellow. Her hair had lost its vitality and was hanging in greasy streaks on her bony shoulders. Her once sumptuous curves that appealed that to Murad, disappeared. At present there was slacking skin, drippy hair and thread-like bones protruding from every corner.

At first she did not recognise him. 'Murad, how are you!'

He stepped in behind her.

'I'm fine,' he said, trying to gain consciousness after having to witness her decaying appearance. 'Where are Mimmy and Lulu?' He noticed their empty beds and the isolated feeling in the room.

'Lulu died to preserve her honour, Mimmy left to barter her honour,' she said. Her voice quivered. She bucked into a tumble of tears. She started to pray, wanting to overthrow the hurricanes of emotion holding her captive. Her heart squeezed itself. She sensed a touch beside her. His face was patiently smiling at her mask of despair. The unspoken language, the communication of love, melted inside of her and oiled the stretched nerves which were clinging to their final threads. She giggled, unable to keep up with the moods her heart was transmitting.

He had made her smile! Murad was always the audience when it came to dealing with Arwa. One day he would stand up from the audience and be the reason for a change in her.

The cruelty imminent in life spiralled around them like a persistent wasp.

'Allah hu Akbar Allah hu Akbar!' The sky parted, waiting for the sun to paint its syrupy glaze on every top, snip and corner.

Sluggish heads slid out of their slumber and got prepared to face their Lord. Families, friends, companions hurried to stand shoulder to shoulder, feet to feet to fall at the foot of His throne.

But *she* had to do it alone. She clutched inwardly, feeling her soul for comfort. She awoke with a partner, Anxiety, and it reared over her every move. The loss of all relationships, all this with life was refilled with the waters of spirituality. Day by day her spiritual foetus would feed on her practices, live on her prayers and excrete her fears. Sometimes it occured to her to leave the palace, but then where would she go? This was her tomb, she was implanted here to be submerged. And, she was ready to sink as deep as she needed to.

Murad had returned from his military training now, and he helped her gradually, day by day to overcome the loss of Mimmy, steering away the grey storm clouds that had gathered about her in a stubbly fuzz. He was a blessing in disguise. Who would have thought that a few months in military training would change him so much. She recalled the clean shaven boy, who was always too tall for his age, and shied away with embarrassment if any female talked to him. So much so that he would leave the room! But now he was a magnificent structure; radiantly bronzed skin covered his strong muscles like a fitted sheet, the long columns of his legs supported the broad bulk of his body and the flat joint between his hips carried an appeal of their own.

They shared a mutual friendship of trust, understanding and support. They were like twins, curled up into one another, surrounded with the salinity of the sands. During the day time, Murad would attend to Atif's plans and Arwa would assist Rawia with the daily chores. In the evenings, between Asir and Magrib prayer they would find one another to talk to about anything. She tried her best to fall into the comfort of silence. He didn't allow it.

Decorated Arabic plates and panels adorned her walls. Large velvety floor cushions detailed with her own bead work coloured the floor. Each day she would customise the environment to wipe out the memory of her deficit. Random placements and arrangements made her feel that she gained rather than lost. Murad urged her to eat, she was starving herself. Silver trays consisted of her three course meal: generous helpings of fish fillets, the head, the tail and general body omitted, saffron smelling rice with an exclusive sac of olive oil for each grain, thick, creamy gravy which was not watered down. So much food, but she was never hungry. The sight filled her up.

One evening, as they were seated together in Arwa's room, her on the bed and him on Mimmy's former bed, he surprised her with a present. 'Arwa, I have been waiting a long time to give you this,' he began. Bashfulness dripped from him in a layer of soft, warm wax.

Arwa cast her brown eyes in his direction.

He was stuttering like a child.

'What's the matter Murad?' She got up and walked towards him.

'No!' He felt the charge in her body come closer. He took

two steps back, so as not to be drawn towards her. His palms clutched the handcuff in his pocket.

She nodded, and went back to her bed.

Murad felt embarrassed. The desire of wanting to capture her in a passionate embrace heightened in his chest like a thunder storm. His limbs ached, trying to tame the pulsating fury of his passion. He longed for a touch to transport him into the world of affection, and to be able to speak the language of love.

Arwa focused her eyes on the windows in the room, then over to the door. He always made it a point to keep the door wide open and refused to see her after dusk. What he did not know was that her love had all dried up, with cracks metres deep.

'Arwa, I bought this for you!' Murad said. He threw a small leather pouch onto her bed.

She picked up the shrivelled up purse.

'Well open it!'

'Murad, what is this?'

A smile hovered about his lips as he lowered his eyes with dignity. 'I have a salary Arwa, but no one to spend it on. This is the first time I have bought a gift, for anyone, please accept it.' He saw her fingers stretch reluctantly, releasing the pouch. 'As a token of our friendship,' he quickly added.

Arwa tipped the contents on to the bed. A beautiful silver kohl case, a silver hand cuff and a comb fell out.

'Why, these are beautiful!' She raised her large brown eyes to meet his. She put on the handcuff and opened the Kohl box. For a moment, she forgot the strain her nerves had kindled for the past few weeks, they vented out with the kind gesture. 'Oh Murad, Shukran!' The teeth in the comb scraped her scalp more than her lifeless hair.

The cool evening breeze refreshed them both, reminding

167

them that it was time for Maghrib prayer.

'I had better take my leave now.' Murad said, glowing secretly at the fact that Arwa had genuinely adored his gifts. An extensive delight skipped playfully in his chest. He sighed. The crux of hope lit up the dark path towards the mosque like fire flies.

Slowly and gradually Arwa would find that they could unleash the concealed compassion they had for each other.

[1] Long Arabian male attire
[2] Yemeni male attire

The Nature Cycle

'Are you purposely ignoring me?'

'Maybe.'

'But why, all I ever did was love you.'

She ignored him. 'I see you have a son.' She froze at the sight of the young boy holding his hand. 'Congratulations,' she wished him, the jealousy peeping through the forced greeting.

'Arwa, please talk to me.'

'There's nothing left to say.' She paused. 'You did all the talking.'

A blankness moulded onto his face like clay.

'You don't get the message do you. I don't suppose you will.' She rolled up her eyes, frustrated. 'Here, take this,' she said, firmly placing a scroll in his hand. 'You will surely get the message now.' Surprised, he opened out the scroll as she disappeared into another row of seats. She was right, by the end of the last word on the page he had grasped the concept firmly by the throat:

> I was a naïve seed, just like another in a myriad,
> But you picked me after a regiment of consideration,
> And planted me into your sweet scented heart,
> With a waterfall of joyful splashing water,
> Supplemented with your cheerful radiant sunshine,
> As I grew to love you too you taught me that I was special,
> The stem grew stronger and sturdier as the relationship bloomed,
> You cuddled up into my outstretched leaves,

Played blissfully with my root-hairs,
Whispered into my bud that I was your glowing temptation,
I danced with the rain and swayed with the wind,
My soft shapely petals were your possessive pride.

But gently the air surrounding us became colder:
Your euphoria of everlasting moisture evaporated,
And your affectionate heat froze,
The singing bright light grew dimmer and duller – you changed,
My roots fought for your soil, for your food; a series of conflicts,
I tried my best to get the tasteful harmony playing afresh,
But it was too late: a bee took my pol-
len of faith from the shrinking bud,
From sheer rejection, my leaves matured into crisp form,
The suffocating pain was unbearable: I dis-
persed all our intimate moments,
Sadly, weakly and heart broken – grain by
grain was released resentfully,
You reduced our once vibrant colourful orchard,
To a shrub in the snow, thirsty for new sunshine.

Chapter 16

An undulating coppery light bathed the white marble of the palace in deep gold. The sharp, smooth towers gleamed like mirrors from a recent rain. The scene was mystical. Lush flowers dipped in morning dew sang their heart out in celebration of a new day. A sea of gold fell like ripples on the courtyard. Puddles of light shrank and skipped with partners on the palace boundaries. The dreamlike essence of the day settled around him.

Atif raised his head from the clumps of coffee samples that lay scattered about on his desk. He was annoyed at his inattentiveness. Intermingled vibes caught him in their desperate force. No matter how hard he tried, the force was irrepressible. He knew he had to submit to it in any case.

For days he had not seen nor made any attempts to meet Arwa, the wild young seamstress who he knew was responsible for this transmutation in him. He recalled how she struck like lightning, her red face and dangerously seductive eyes catching his heart. She was the wounded agony that he entombed within himself, which he had never allowed to escape from the clutches of his thriving heart. Until now

He felt the coolness of the air in his nostrils. He let it flow freely in his head, leaning back against his chair thinking about their effusive encounter. He smiled unconciously as his emotions crusaded him away, thinking that he should at least go and visit Arwa and thank her for this relief. Since she was not making dolls anymore she would need a new task. He motioned to one of the fanning boys. 'Kindly find Rawia and ask her to come to my office.'

The thin, pale complexioned boy scampered off to obey the order.

Rawia arrived many hours later, walking upright and elegantly as usual with a bundle in one hand. She had plaited her hair differently, the two plaits clinging perfectly and symmetrical to the sides of her head like silver calligraphy engraved on a plaque. Even her usual dress was more vibrant, peeking through her loosely draped black veil. To the formalities of the approaching evening, Rawia made the concession of changing from her loose, weary uniform to a fitted green dress, and from turning her hair from a neat bun into an elaborate style. In addition, she had even scented her body with jasmine oil which cycloned out from her in bewildering cross-currents. You did not see Rawia tonight. You *sensed* her.

'Assalamoalaikum Rawia.' Atif greeted her without looking up.

'Walaikum Assalam.' The words bounced on waves from her heart, not from her throat.

He lifted his eyes, trailing them upwards from her feet to her head. Noticing the stark contrast to her usual sober appearance, he commented: 'Any special occasion?'

The soothing pleasure of him noticing her efforts caused her heart to flutter so hard that she thought she could hear it knocking against her ribs. 'Not really Sheikh Atif, I felt like a change, that's all.' To her disappointment, he didn't make any further comments about her leafy green dress or the new way she had braided her hair, instead he handed her a bundle. She consoled herself in her usual manner, viewing his nature as masculine and dignified. She focused on the thick cover of the hair on his head.

'Arwa the seamstress, do you remember her?'

'Why I practically mothered her Sir.'

'Has she recovered from the loss of her friend?'

'She is wading her way through it at her own pace.'

'Good.' He leaned over to his shisha and filled it with rose flavoured tobacco. 'I would like you to send her to me please. I have a new task for her. We must keep her occupied so that she does not plunge so deep into sadness that she becomes incapable of swimming back up to the surface.'

The gems on the chandeliers hummed like the wings of a parade in the insect kingdom.

She looked at him inquiringly. 'Yes, I will send her to you right away.' Rawia clutched the bundle in her right arm so tightly and nervously that her nails almost pierced the rich silk.

'Sheikh Atif....'

'Yes Rawia?'

For a moment their eyes met, but she shied away. 'I have sewn another bedspread for your room. Shall I change the ones presently there?'

'Do what pleases you Rawia,' he said, in between sucks of the tobacco smoke. The more he felt unburdened, the more Rawia would load him with unnecessary things.

Rawia watched his strong lips loop around the mouth pipe. The soft flesh suckled the opening so gently, so sophisticatedly. Delighted that as usual, she was granted the authority over the interior design in his bedroom, she went to call Arwa. One day she would have an authority in his life.

They said Rawia was good with her hands. She healed people with her fingers, finding exact points and stimulating them with warm pressure. As a side business, and to prevent herself from totally merging into the walls of the palace, she treated people who had aches and pressing health conditions. Despite the stashes of compliments she received at each session she found, to her aggravation, she could not cure herself. Days, nights, decades she had spent within the confines of the palace, but even then she really did not know why she felt an emptiness. It was hollow and consuming her inside out. Over the years this uncertainty grew onto her face, so she just wore a permanent mask to conceal it. Even her eyes were part of her human theatre; they would not reveal their restlessness to anyone. She mastered her body, she mastered her mind, she mastered her heart. She stepped into the seamstress' room.

Arwa was busy reading the Qur'an. She recited it softly and fluently, such that her voice resonated like a young bird, humming her morning song, filling the intervals of silence with a spiritual conversation. Rawia stood silently, flattered by the progress that Arwa had made. She leaned against a chair whilst the utterances poured into her system too. The empty beds once occupied by Mimmy and Lulu were now sprawling and spreading with the holy shield that Arwa had created around her. At first, Rawia shuddered at this observation, but then she relaxed, upon reflection that Arwa was reaching an inner peace.

'Arwa, Assalamoalaikim.'

'Walaikum Assalaam,' Arwa whispered, eyeing the abstract quality imminent in Rawia's usually subdued appearance. She normally looked like a functionary of the palace, but today she resembled an expensive, elaborate art sculpture, which could slot into any wedge in the palace.

Rawia laughed. 'Oh, you must be wondering why I am all made up,' she said jovially, striding across to the small mirror on the back wall. 'Well I just felt like a change, my dear. Sometimes one feels they have played a part too long, to the extent that they begin to lose the colour in their identity. I just wanted to slip into a fresh transition, which I hope will give birth to a never ending rainbow.' Then silently, to herself she thought: I've always worn black or white. It's time to taste the colours, their pigments, their textures and their combinations. She blushed a shade of cherry pink at the image which sprang to her mind, at what she hoped would be at the other end of the rainbow.

Arwa lowered her eyes, suddenly conscious that her stares must be making the woman feel quite uncomfortable. 'I hope you find a nice surprise at the other end of your rainbow.'

'It's not a surprise I am travelling towards,' Rawia said, as she spinned around to face Arwa. 'I know what I want.'.

Arwa became tired within the wisps of the complicated discussion. She drew herself out, uninterested. 'Was there a particular task for me?'

'Ah yes, Sheikh Atif wanted to see you about that. He will tell you about your new duties.'

'Well why didn't he just instruct you, like he normally does? Why does he want to see me personally?' Her nerves mustered together at the prospect of meeting the blunt, choppy personality of the young sheikh again.

To her incredulity, Rawia discovered that she had no answer, which was exceptional since she could usually answer for him.

Arwa left, leaving her to ponder about the correct explanation.

Coffee formulated the essence of the pride that festered in the palace from behind every corner. With each step closer to Sheikh Atif's office, the burnt-ash reek grew stronger, thickening the air like a cloth. Its position had been made apparent to Arwa in a social affair not long ago. Rawia had been busily arranging a generous platter for the attendees, when she requested Arwa's help. Arwa helped to make the rose syrup concoction that was served to all of Sheikh Atif's guests. She swirled the rose syrup and milk together, and frothed the cream. Next, she sprinkled a handful of mixed nuts; pine nuts, pistachios and roasted cashews to make it crunchy. The last item that was placed on the trolley was a cupful of powdery coffee beans, uncovered and set on the bottom shelf. Arwa was flummoxed as to why this part of the arrangement was left unfinished prior to the guests arrival. Surely the Sheikh would not grind the beans himself! Rawia advised her that Atif would crush, grate and roast the coffee himself. It was considered a very big insult to offer previously prepared coffee to a guest. Since then, Arwa had concluded that the permanent ashy stench in the upper floor of the palace was because the young sheikh was very popular.

The young sheikh offered her a seat.

'Shukran,' whispered Arwa.

There was something strange about the palace that evening. Like Rawia, his bronzed complexion was glowing as well. The vibes he emitted were snaky, more sinuous and very targeted. Arwa sat awkwardly, compacting herself as much as she could, far too aware that her master's eyes were tightly focused on her. It was an unpleasant feeling since she didn't know where they were wandering.

Atif wanted to stare at her face, but whenever their eyes would meet his body was so hot with the charge her brown discs emitted, that he swore his skin burned. So he let his eyes drop down a bit. She had a nice trim body, not obese, nor underfed. Just right. Each breast was in proportion, like soft, juicy peaches. Then he felt the burning ice tap him again, he let his eyes drop down further in guilt. Her hands, they were delicate and laced to-

176

gether in her lap. Thin, feminine fingers wrapped themselves over one another, cushioned between her firm thighs. He wondered what her legs looked like, whether they were thin or firm, rounded or fat, olive or fair, soft or rough?

It was best to focus his eyes somewhere else. It was too easy to get lost in her curvy landscape. So he decided to look at everything, but her.

He spoke eventually, after focusing an awkward amount of time on the skirting in the corner of the room. 'Taking into account the recent events which have occurred in the palace, I have a new task planned for you.' Without looking at her, he sensed her sitting as rigid as pottery moulded to dry at the other end of the room. 'I would like you to sew dresses.' He waited for a response to the proposition.

Silence reacted for her. Her stone-like attitude made him smile. She had such soft, humble features; curly hair, large captivating eyes and a small, plump mouth. As his passions surged higher, she suddenly broke the hovering feeling that she had long been suppressing.

'Of course Sheikh Atif. You must tell me the measurements and colours for I cannot begin without knowing the size,' she said. Her eyelids hooded over her warm nutty eyes like a tent mounted on a falling cliff.

Unconsciously, his shining face radiated with delight. He was dumbfounded.

'The size?' Her eyes focussed on his hands that were clasped quite tightly together behind his back at the other end of the room.

'Your size!' he blurted out, as if he had received a medal of some sort.

'My size?'

'Your size,' he repeated. His heart quivered with delight as he imagined her in a pure white lace outfit, luminous and pure as a freshly peeled pearl out of a shell. He turned to face her.

Involuntarily she stiffened. What was he suggesting? Rousing herself from the contemplation, she elevated her eyes to meet his. Curved hooks at the ends of both pair of eyes drew their ropes tighter. Something moved inside of her, and she knew it was her heart. It needed to be fed with affection. She slipped out of her wary crouch, recognising the fairytale she was creating around her. 'When would you like them *sir?*'

Unconsciously rubbing his lips together, Atif threw more tension into the atmosphere. 'Whenever you are ready. Take your time. Make them any design you like.' He narrowed his eyes. 'After all, they are for a very special person.'

She concluded that she did not want to be a part of this ridiculous conversation any longer. She gathered her dress and stood up.

His heart leapt violently at the sight of the silver anklet around her slender white ankle. Rambling with pleasure he darted to obstruct her course, coasting at a stop near the door.

'What are you doing?' Her eyes widened at the intrusion.

Pricking his ears to ensure that there was no one about to witness the rupture of his endurance, he lowered his face to hers, close enough that she could feel the tiny hairs on her face tinge in his heat. She immediately took a step back so that she was leaning against the door, bewildered at his outrageous behaviour. To her amazement, he caged her from all sides within the contours of his musky flavoured chest.

'Forgive me for being so brazen. But I have to tell you something of a great magnitude. If I don't, my heart will surely burst.' There wasn't time to ponder on the choice or order of his words.

Arwa was backed into a tight corner; she tried to step into the hardness of the door behind her so that her breasts would not brush against his panting chest. They rubbed each other in a dance. 'Let me leave.' She wanted to escape, but simultaneously she was aware that these set of actions enticed her in a weird and wonderful way.

'Leave? But I love you Arwa. Since the day you unravelled the wicked web cocooning my soul, I realised for the first time a shapeless sensation in my life. A shapeless sensation which I long to define forever in your embrace.' He lowered his face to align his eyes with her hiding ones. 'I love you,' he whispered into her mouth.

The line reverberated in her consciousness. Not knowing how to react, she laughed. In the beginning it was out of modesty, but as the words repeated themselves in her head, the laughter curled into the shape of a fact. Her! She could never be a lady of this mansion, what was the sheikh thinking?

'Are you drugged?'

There was no reply. His eyelashes sunk low, blowing his humiliation off onto the floor in flakes.

To her horror, it was true! He really *did* love her. Wanting to ease him out of the illusion, she stared directly and honestly into his longing eyes. 'I am flattered Sheikh Atif, but you deserve better. I am not of your kind.'

'Islam is colour blind.'

'You forget you may be colour blind but everyone else has been blessed with perfect sight,' she said. Her lips pursed and a frown hung itself from one end of her head to the other. 'I must leave now.' She stomped towards the exit.

'What do you mean? What is your religion Arwa?'

'My religion is only what benefits me. I was taught that by

179

Fate a long time ago.'

Upset that his words did not achieve the effect that he perceived, he put his hand into the pocket of his thobe, cradling a tiny velvety pouch between his fingers. 'Wait Arwa, take this,' he said. He took her small fist and forced it open. He placed the pouch in her palm, and closed her fingers over the present firmly.

Overcome by the wave that heightened and crashed powerfully at his touch, she leapt away from him in the direction of her room.

ᘓ ᘓ ᘓ ᘓ ᘓ ᘓ ᘓ ᘓ ᘓ ᘓ

The traditional craft of deriving beauty from the benefits of nature was one of Arwa's thriving interests in the palace. Back in Rawda village, girls of her age dwelled on nature expeditions. They were professional experts at selecting and combining ingredients to ensure the best result. Arwa always went on her expeditions alone, venturing on marshland and mountain plains by herself because she had no friends. Spices and leaves, fruit slices and vegetable seeds were mixed together to produce cooling foot gels, wrinkle reducing face masks and nourishing hair conditioners. In the palace, nature divorced itself and was located at the other end of the world.

One day Arwa offered to dye Rawia's hair for her, into a rich shade of burgundy. She convinced her that it would improve the quality of her locks. She had to keep herself occupied, since there was no more Lulu or Mimmy to pass time with. Rawia eventually agreed, comparing the vitality inherent in Arwa's looks and her own fading beauty, and thus arranged for the ingredients to be brought directly to the seamstress' room.

Arwa was excited. A sapling thrill branched out onto the surface of her skin. Although the attraction of collecting her own ingredients was absent, she carried the sensation forward, concentrating on the task. Sadly, the ingredients arrived powdered and ready to mix, further disillusioning her, since her task was easier but less fulfilling. Placing a large bowl on the table, she opened each of the cloth packets and tipped them in. She added one cup of henna powder, half a cup of coffee powder and half a cup of gooseberry juice to bind the mixture together. She fused them into a reddish-brown paste, and added half a cup of coconut for nourishment, half a cup of beetroot juice for conditioning and three drops of eucalyptus oil to reduce the effect of headaches. She scraped the dye into an iron vessel for a few hours, so that it would deepen in colour.

When the paste was ready to use, she inhaled it, letting the rusty, mushroomy, earthy feel infuse her blood. Arwa smeared it on Rawia's head, spreading it in lengths along wedges of her hair. Finally she wrapped her head in a cloth, until the paste-cap would dry up and crack, signalling that it was ready to wash off.

Her hair now softer, conditioned and much stronger, Rawia was impressed with the results. But most of all it enhanced her appearance. She would not let the girl's talent go to waste. She appointed Arwa as her daily beauty advisor, creating a diversion for both of them for a few days.

Rawia very soon became obsessed. She required a honey-oat mask everyday, an exfoliating bean scrub every other day and a face sculpting massage weekly. Arwa was tired; keeping up with Rawia's increasing requests drained her. Results were gradual, not in a sudden explosive burst, which was clearly Rawia's expectation. She attempted to get the message through to the old lady, but nothing made a difference.

Rawia was still young, and she wanted to be able to believe in this fact herself.

Chapter 17

Murad shook the major's hand briefly and gave a solemn salute to his men. The next few days were going to be difficult: training, camping and sweating under the shadows of nature's ancient ruins. He would soon become a Sergeant Major himself.

He wanted to see Arwa before he left. Now, back in his cabin, he unconsciously put on his uniform. He wasn't quite sure why he tended to wear the army attire every time he went to meet her, he just knew that he looked worthy. While he was arranging his sash he smiled without realising it. He was going to work hard, extra hard to become a Sergeant Major and then he would be worthy of Arwa's love. Lying down on his bed he closed his hot eyes.

An image of her slender cream complexion draped in sheets of ruby red velvet triggered a compassionate ache in his chest. Before he could consider their farewell scene, his thoughts were scattered by the marching of squads and a chorus of hoof beats outside. Surprised, he looked out of his window – why were the troops assembling at this hour? As far as he recalled they were to leave after Maghrib prayer.

Observing the urgency of the situation he gathered his things and raced to Arwa's room. She was busy snipping fabric as he barged in, the cuts falling to the floor around her toes. He hastily straightened himself, discomfited by the lack of style in his entrance, ironing out any fresh creases with his fingers. 'Assalamo-alaikum Arwa.'

'Walaikum Assalam,' she replied, her eyes expressing vivacity.

Forming a mental image of her before him, he lowered his gaze, and conveyed the reason for his sudden departure.

'That's wonderful Murad! Make sure you work very hard. Allah will reward you for your efforts,' she said. She put her tailoring aside and made her way towards him. She knew what success meant to him, and his new drive inspired her also.

A flash of ecstasy brewed in his chest as she came closer. Unable to estimate how he would react to her being so near to his inflaming blood, he stumbled backwards on the spears on his boots. His heart took flight, he wanted to lunge out at her, but a tension was multiplying in his head. Exhausted by the intoxicating instincts that her presence was having over him, he purged himself out of the unbearable position: 'Well I must leave now. I just wanted to let you know that I was leaving, I'll be back in a week or so.'

She raised her eyes to meet his (although he cleverly shielded them by turning his head away) noticing the lofty ambition brimming feverishly in him. 'That is very kind of you. I wish you the best of luck,' she said before he disappeared in the direction of the assembly in the grounds.

Arwa laughed to herself, resuming her position underneath the pile of white silks and lace that Atif had sent to her room. A huge multicoloured dome formed of aspirations rose high in her head. Noticeably, she felt peaceful and happier. She was not sure if she had accepted Atif's invitation to step ahead into a relationship together. He appeared to be sincere and was obviously unlike his psychological father. But could it all be a farce? How could she, a simple seamstress even be considered to be a principle part of this superior wonderland? More importantly, could she play the part? It was not her, she would have to *become* it.

Her attention diverted to the pouch Atif had given her the night before. She pulled it out of her special place, the antique jewellery box. Initially, she had repeatedly considered if it was worthy of its placement amongst her greatest memories, but after feeling the strange consciousness which sprouted from each word on the scroll she knew that she felt something else too, a mysterious magnetism towards a living creature that she had never felt before. Her heart spoke to her in abrupt bursts of energy, informing her that it was happy. Wanting to be lifted upon the looming clouds again, she excitedly unrolled the scroll. It read:

The Perfect Pictorial

Glimpsing myself in the doublet mystical spheres,
A peaceful alluring, comforting imprison-
ment; where I wade within tears,
The key to which just melts away,
Suspended, in the divine kingdom I float astray.

But when the glistening hazelnuts burn ablaze,
They force fierce icicles into a haze,
Trembling, I crouch to think what I have done,
Waiting for that cheerful bright light to return to my sun.

I remember the fondling, caressing, protecting,
Moulding me beautifully free – yet tingling,
To surf in the aura, attraction, the intimate fusion,
Entangling me further into fanatical illusion.

Where the occasion arises when the cocoon unravels,
The smooth fragile lawyers swift away on their travels,

Friction encapsulates tensely tender refinement,
Again, souls are poured into vessels for replenishment.

The invigorating passion, a provocative permeability,
Quadruple sponges – a path to tranquillity,
Absorbing into each other – a singular creation,
Unable to resist the tantalising invitation.

Sometimes I fear that it will not be there,
All those guilt trips will drive nothing to share,
But the magical colander resting gently on coloured frustrations,
Will never lose its touch, but simply nourish simplifications.

The tasteful relaxing fragrance of seducing spirits,
Who sail the skies mocking physical attraction,
One another's meaningful, shapeless presence, inhibits-
Our sole legend: the all in all interaction.

Unconvinced that she understood all of it, she knew that she still wanted to taste the fruit of his exertions towards her, after all, he wrote her a poem! It was a fact that every person that she had ever loved had dissipated within what appeared to resemble a few hours. She was a captive, a slave of the conniving mendacity which had encapsulated her for the past years. It always took the same route and she was tired of it: a mellifluousness vent would echo its peacefulness into a new picture, and then acid droplets of reality would eat away the illusion.

All she knew was that she did not want to be calloused any further. Mesmerised by the show of his affections, she drew out the contents of the pouch. It was a thick, chunky gold brace-let encrusted with watery green emeralds. It was breathtakingly beautiful. She felt the precision of the polished jewels with her forefinger. Smooth metal and silken stone. She slipped it on her wrist. The bracelet adorned her in a beauty like the first stars peeping through the blinding dust of the desert gales.

Arwa wanted to congregate with him, to thank him for the gift but she did not know how. The other servants would spy on her, suspect something and report to Sheikh Khalil. She stroked her throat, hoping to soothe the obstruction that attempted to choke her. Even if Atif did approve of it, a steepening fear lingered between her ribs because Khalil could disapprove of her background. After all, she was a Muslim now, but she had been a Jewess. A Jewess from a family whose father sold his children. Her mother was a harlot (it didn't matter how she justified it, she would always be stained as a woodlouse of society). She would not reveal her past to anyone, the thorns would scratch her out once and for all. Self-respect and maintaining honour was important at any cost— that was a fact. Lulu killed herself for the sake of it, Lulu's father swapped his own daughter to maintain it. So honour was definitely important. Unless, of course, she intended to weave her destiny into the likes of Mimmy or Lulu. As she picked up the bodice of the dress she had designed, she felt the richness of the fabric flow smoothly between her fingers. Fitted according to her own size, she placed it on the manikin to attach the ribbons along the waist. This will accentuate my waist, she thought, as she imagined herself wrapped between the layers of silk and lace. Though she was a learner at sewing dresses for real people rather than small dolls, one could not tell that she was a beginner at all. Her dexterity was amazing. Everything was perfectly proportioned and she ensured that the correct fabric was used to achieve a striking effect.

Whilst she was pinning the ribbons into place, the red protruding stone on the silver handcuff became entangled within the pearl studded lace sleeves. She carefully tackled out the ensnared threads so as not to ruin the lace. As she was twisting the stubborn thread out of the corner of a ridge of the handcuff, there was a knock at the door.

'Come in.'

A black servant boy stepped in, his skin as smooth and velvety as creamy lentil granules. 'The young Sheikh asked me to deliver this to you.' He held out a small scarlet pouch evidently drenched in rose perfume.

'Leave it on the bed,' Arwa said. She tried her best not to reveal the exorbitant tremor lifting up inside her.

The messenger put the pouch on the bed and left the room.

Arwa pounced on the pouch. Her electrified fingers trembled as she loosened the strips of satin. Inside, lay a small scroll which was no longer than the span of her palm. Spreading it out, it read:

> My beloved Arwa,
> Meet me by the well when the moon shines bright.
> Your admirer and friend,
> Atif.

It was written in the same delicate calligraphy as the poem, the only difference being that the flicks were more aggressive, as if it had been scribbled in a hurry. Rolling it back up, she wondered what she should wear for their midnight encounter. She wanted to look special, but not desperate like those serpent-like harem girls. An icy quiver rolled down her spine as she recalled the amorous assassinations she had witnessed on that cursed night. From the window the moonlight spilled in, like the luminous tendency of the shiny surface of a milky lake. Arwa dressed up in her best outfit, a lilac dress that she had embroidered with silver sequins for Eid the previous year. On her shoulders she wore a sheer shawl that she extended to cover her head with. The spray of sequins on the net scarf looked like diamonds against her dark tousled curls showing from underneath: the starry night was trapped and encapsulated on her head. She outlined her eyes with the kohl powder to intensify the expression of her gaze. Her look was complete. In the mirror she did not recognise the reflection that stood exquisitely in front of her. If she wanted, her range had the capacity to be unbelievable. Silently, she drew her black purdah over herself, and went out to meet her admirer amongst the drapes of the black night.

A scum covered ditch obstructed her path that night, chameleons arranging into a splash of jagged colour around it. They feasted upon the astonishing view: the iridescent turquoise blue vacillating into a deep sea green. Against the cliché of the palace, the sight was exotic, almost maddening. But Arwa was attracted to it, tempted by the originality of the sequence.

Atif waited patiently for his beloved by the well, watching the moon high in the sky stare back at him. When he heard soft footsteps drawing closer, his chest quaked with delight. The well was situated outside the entrance to the palace so there was no danger of anyone invading their bubble of bliss. 'You came!' he said, almost as if he did not expect her to do so.

'I wanted to thank you for the gift.' A gentle breeze blew the black cloak off her head, revealing the lilac net scarf that covered her hair.

The hole in the well silently filled up.

At the sight of her enchanting image, Atif felt his heart leap. 'You look beautiful.'

Arwa blushed tenderly at the compliment. and lined her head to gaze into his eyes. His beard had been trimmed, revealing his sculpted jaw and he had perfumed himself with musk. The visual and physical assault affected her senses. 'Shukran,' she said under her breath.

His hand drew through the tendrils that softened the absorptive quality of her face. He pulled her gently down beside him and they sat leaning against the well. He fondled her in intricate movements, with voice, touch and gaze. They were surrounded by the mild sound of the wind sliding over the surface of the water in the well, and the crystal intensity of the moonlit air around them.

Unfamiliar with any embrace, Arwa tried to maintain her distance. After all, he may be in love with her, but she did not know if *she* had tipped into the ocean of love yet.

'I apologise. It seems as if a hurricane blows me away when I am around you. Don't be scared.' His voice dropped further. 'Soon we will not have to meet like this, you will be my wife.'

Enveloped in silence, she managed to confront her fears. 'Atif I am an employee. Your father will never accept me—'

He unexpectedly twisted towards her and placed a teak finger against her waxy lips. It infuriated her. How could he just touch her like that? It was obscene.

'When Allah is the only authority to accept and forgive anything who is my father to intrude?'

'But…' she said from behind his finger. She pushed it away his harshly in one blow with her hand. If he wanted to argue, then fine. She was untouchable. She was not married yet.

'No. We are all equal Arwa. It would be better if your mind was not plagued with such primitive thoughts.' He noticed that her eyes were searching for a fight, it was best to ignore it.

Lightening his tone he praised the bracelet. 'Do you know it was my mothers? I always kept it as a memory, my father got rid of all the rest of her jewels, sold them and gave them away to charity. This, was for my wife.'

The anger in her eyes soothed itself and streamed out into the open. 'I am honoured that you found me worthy of such a privilege,' she said, 'but really I am not perfect.'

He commanded her to look at him. She fell headfirst into an entrapment of feeling that cleaved around them. For quite a while they sat there, statues moulded out of desire for one another restricted forcefully by the snapping bands of self-control.

Arwa finally broke the silence, ahead of them becoming entombed in the concordant magic of the moment. 'Atif if we are to begin a relationship you must know the truth about me.'

'I do not want to know about it and I do not care.'

'But you told me about yourself,' she said.

'Only tell me if your heart wants to open up, for me it makes no difference. I am indifferent to whatever you choose or have chosen in the past for yourself,' he said. His eyes stirred in the moonlit sky, bobbing in the boat to Fantasy Island.

His frankness stimulated a courage within her, strong enough in its force to release the fear she had long been surpessing since her first step into the palace. She lowered her eyes. 'It's my turn to confess. Atif, my real name is not Arwa. It is Sara. I changed it when I arrived here to preserve my identity as a Jew.'

'A Jew!' His eyes widened. Surely, he *had* seen her pray.

'Yes, a Jew.'

'But Sara is the name of our prophet Abraham's wife . You did not need to change it.'

'I did not know at the time that Islam follows the same beliefs as Judaism. I was only fifteen when myself and my sister were sold by my father as slaves.' She paused, feeling tears seeping into the lower buckets of her eyes. 'My sister left me for the life of those illicit harem girls that your father indulges in, Lulu left her life for honour and I only recently converted fully to Islam.' The last few words pushed over the splurging buckets.

Compelled to put a comforting arm around the sobbing girl, he tried to relieve her pain. Both of them were survivors. 'Arwa, as I said I do not care about your past and I still am not affected now that I am aware of it. All that matters is that you are mine and I am yours and that we maintain a state of happiness and harmony.'

She felt the gallop of his love beating loudly into her ear, it was so loud that she felt as if she was riding on it. What was she doing? She was not supposed to touch unlawful men! Flinching a quick glance at his white robe before she pulled away from his embrace, she smiled. 'Atif, Shukran. You are an angel.' Danger did not threaten her anymore. She almost wanted it to steer herself into its clasp and challenge it.

Atif smiled, recovering from his sudden retreat. 'Well this angel has the imprint of precious tears on his chest now,' he said, pointing out the black stains from the liquidised kohl over his robe. It splodged into a peculiar emblem, resembling mating beetles.

'I am so sorry,' Arwa said.

'Your tears are like diamonds for me,' he said. He wanted to nuzzle into her once again but she stood up, her face flushed.

'I fear Allah, Atif. I think we should leave now.' Astonished by her unanticipated withdrawal, Atif understood that she was correct.

'Tomorrow?'

'We'll see,' she replied, her face shining.

The next morning, Arwa stretched across her bed. Rawia had instructed her to help make Sheikh Khalil's breakfast since one of the cooks was taken ill. She jumped out of bed, cloaked in a daze of emotions. She splashed water from her rose pool and blotted her face dry. She got ready chirpily, motivated for the day ahead. As she walked, she noticed the difference in her stride: it was a skip rather than a step each time. She had been seduced by the love ghost. She pushed the door open to the kitchen.

'Oh Arwa, I am so glad you have arrived. It seems that two more of the cooks have been showing symptoms of a fever, we are very short.' Rawia's cheeks streaked red from the stress. Even the tip of her nose was tinged with a deep shade of magenta. 'Sheikh Khalil has been taken ill you see, so he requires a special broth and goodness from vegetables. We are preparing it according to the instructions of the Hakim secretly because the Master refuses to see a Hakim.'

'Why doesn't he want to see the Hakim? Does Atif know that we are doing this?'

Rawia overheard the slip of her tongue. '*Sheikh* Atif,' she said, 'told me personally yesterday. He always tells me first about anything.' She announced this proudly to even the utensils in the kitchen.

Taking the haft end of a small mallet, Arwa tenderised the lamb steaks. Blood juices splurged onto the table. This isn't healthy, she thought, it is much too rich to digest in illness. She pointed this out to Rawia, but apparently Sheikh Khalil favoured the bloody taste. It is his belief that its strength improves the composition of his own thinning blood.' Arwa still did not fully agree, but since they were her elders they might know better.

The other servants shook their heads with irritation. 'There

193

she goes again,' said the girl next to Arwa so suddenly, that the knife slipped out of her hand. Arwa bent to pick it up. Then something which should not have happened, did. The servant girl commented on the bracelet that was on her wrist, eyeing it with interest. 'That's a beautiful bracelet I must say! Extremely expensive!'

Another male servant put some chopped carrots on their counter. 'Looks familiar.' he said, and then walked away.

Arwa covered it up before anyone else noticed. How *could* she have been so naïve?

'Hey, does it not resemble the paintings of the former Mistress Noha, Ahad?' the irritating girl said, her voice so shrill that everyone in the expansive kitchen overheard the echoes, including the skinned chickens heaped in the corner.

Ahad nodded, preoccupied with peeling turnip tops.

Sweat sprinted down the back of Arwa's tinged neck. Afraid that their secret would be revealed, she made an excuse to leave for the washroom and sought permission from Rawia. She sighed with relief when it was granted. As she shut the door, she realised that even more stupidly, she had left the best part of the conversation behind her.

Chapter 18

Atif nuzzled into Arwa's neck with his spongy lips. The wind flowed in a channel between them, light patches of warm air kissing everything they passed. The moon tilted, tipping a layer of milky light over the sea. Black shiny ebony transformed into a chain of shimmering white pearls.

At first, no one stopped them and it slowly blossomed into a ritual for the two of them. Many days would be spent frantically anticipating a midnight debate. Their bodies worked in an opposing routine, a few hours of sleep pumped further adrenaline into their systems. They even met on days when the next morning would be scheduled with a crucial military ceremony. Sometimes their cold exhausted bodies demanded rest, but they sacrificed all to let their hearts fuse for a bit longer.

They talked about being strangers, even to the people they loved. But, in the intimacy of their togetherness, they discussed her dreams, his business, and they joked about the way she slept. Peals of laughter hugged them both. He read out tender lines of poetry to her. She wanted to impress him with her own stanzas, but thought it would be better after marriage so that her written Arabic was more fluent. Rushed emotion did not suit her.

The milky fog at the crack of dawn transported them back to Earth. When raindrops pricked her, he would soothe her. When his shoulders tightened, she loosened them. They fitted together like an egg and its shell. (That's the way Atif described their relationship). Playful arguments would follow at who was the egg and who was the shell, but they never reached an agreement, so they decided each was a bit of both. Together, they discovered an enthusiasm for life that had laid dormant in each of them for a long time.

During their midnight encounters she wished he would not draw so close to her, the uncomfortable, guilty feeling was always there, simmering in her belly, never fully cooked.

'You did not have to get me anything Atif. Our affections for one another do not need to be symbolised by such objects.' She looked at the perfume bottle he had placed in her lap. She paused to look up at his face behind her. 'As long as you feel something here,' she gently pressed his palm against her bosom, 'that is all the gratification I need.' She stepped a little ahead of him, anticipating an embrace in full swing.

His heated green stare searched hers and witnessed her love for him reflected there. Oh Arwa, he thought, do you not see and feel how I want to delve deep into paradise with you? Why are you so hot and cold?

'Atif, I believe in preserving myself for you when we are halal[1] for one another. Patience is greatly rewarded.' She felt quite pleased to be the first to make such an assertion. Her belly deflated.

The pungent saline aroma of the briny sea blew into their faces.

'Arwa accept this. I have chosen it especially for you.' He unwrapped the green silk to reveal a beautiful golden headband with a large diamond shaped emerald to lie at the tip of her forehead. With one hand he cupped her slender neck and with the other he placed the jewellery on her head. 'You resemble an ancient goddess,' he said, speaking as lightly as feathers blowing against her skin.

The sensation of his touch against her skin slapped her dumbfound.

'It will match your bracelet,' he said. He reached for her wrist to show her, but all he found was a wide silver hand cuff which she always seemed to have on. 'Arwa, where is the bracelet? Why did you take it off?'

'I had to Atif. People began to notice and get suspicious. I will wear it all the time once we are married.'

'So why do you always wear this?' He flicked the handcuff with this finger. 'How come you never take this off?'

'I see no reason to take it off, this demonstrates nothing that I must conceal.' She slipped in front of his turned back. 'Don't be offended, if you want me to wear it I will.' She encircled his waist with her arms, unwillingly, but out of love. 'But don't expect me to wear this headband all the time!' She laughed as he turned towards her in the embrace.

Atif pressed her into himself, wanting his mouth to assault hers, but withdrew before he got carried away. 'I apologise my darling, I wanted you to like it. For a moment I thought you had another admirer.' He looked into her eyes and sensed despair, a hollowness that he knew only he filled in some strange way.

'Another admirer?'

'Yes.' He looked away, the jealousy hunching his posture.

'Why?'

'Because you never remove that handcuff.' He cleared his throat in embarrassment.

Arwa watched the little boy step into the prince's darkly aristocratic aura. The opposition in his masculinity and his innocence lured her further towards him. 'This was from a friend. It does not hold enough value to what you have given me.' She looked shyly at the floor. 'Nothing ever has touched me this way, and nothing ever will.'

Their emotions stirred violently as he urged her to take his hand and walk towards the camel caravan. As they rode back to the palace she leaned into his chest sleepily.

'Atif, I love you,' she whispered.

Amazed at this first public announcement of her feelings for him, he stretched his hand to draw it through her heaped curls. But then he stopped. If he truly loved her, he could wait. Wait! How annoying that word sounded, especially to a man of his status. This was his test, he was failing it, and he was more than aware of it. There was no reward without a test. It slashed him in the heart, their marriage would have to be soon, as soon as Abati recovered.

The camel caravan stopped a little before it reached the palace so that no one could witness their entrance. As usual, Atif would take the main gate and Arwa would take the back door to the courtyard. He gently ruffled her hair to wake her up. Each curl bounced against another invitingly, maintaining its coil.

Jolting out of her slumber she hopped out of the caravan. She was embarrassed that she had drifted away into sleep, but humiliated that after all that talk about patience, *she* had oozed herself in his arms. He must think she was a hypocrite!

'No need to behave like a frog, my sweetness. You were tired,' he said, straightening his robe as he stepped out of the caravan. 'And I must admit I enjoyed it as much as you did as you slid into a drowsy rest. I wish I could savour the moment forever.'

Quadruple eyes tangled themselves into a knot. Their tongues were ecstatic with the pleasure that dripped down from the stare, wanting to rub up against one another.

A cocktail of electric blue-green flies became a solid obstacle for their return. She guessed that they were attracted to the gorgeous green jewel upon her head. Later, she derived that their prime enticement was the coconut conditioning oil in her hair.

Glowing at her admirer's hot whispers into her ear, Arwa led the way back to the palace. She turned a final time before they parted routes, of servant and master, to catch a glimpse of him until the following night. She turned the corner leading to the backdoor. As she approached the brown rusted latch, she dabbed some oil into the hinges so that they would not creak. She stepped cautiously inside the palace grounds, shutting the door behind her ever so quietly, making out in the direction of her room.

A brightly coloured Agamid lizard keeled over in fright as Arwa loosened a window shutter. She wasn't scared, since they were frequent visitors in the village, creating a dynamic three dimensional mural on the wall. Poor creature, she thought, as it moved away from the deflecting pane. Arwa wanted to show it the directions back to its own home, but she did not how to. Ten years had passed without her setting foot into the outside world, not because she was denied a trip, but because she was petrified of being bartered again. Rawda Village was as isolated from her, as she was from any hope of locating it. Both her and the lizard were on an exclusive island, trying to find their own kind. She had found her own kind, and she wished that the lizard would too.

Tired, restless eyes were gazing out of the window. It was still a few hours till Fajr prayer and her turbulent nerves did not allow her to sleep. Rawia could not help being affected by the chitter chatter in the kitchen, she felt her heart muffle and weep inside her rib cage. It wanted to escape. If the bracelet *was* the former Mistress' then Atif had taken affection towards Arwa. A tear scratched down her face and thudded to the ground.

She clenched her teeth in anger. It was true that she had

mothered the girl but she could never have imagined she would betray her like this! Why, she was not even his age – she was much younger! If anyone was suitable for his masculine charms it was Rawia, who waited and served him over the years. He told *her* everything not Arwa. He confided in her, *she* was capable of fulfilling his needs, no one else. She was the closest to him. Even today, she spent the entire day nursing Sheikh Khalil for Atif's sake. Surely he noticed her efforts? Extra position needed extra patience, needed extra time.

Her thoughts halted as she sighted a small figure stealing in between the shadows of the courtyard. It was covered in a black purdah, but the head was adorned with a jewel.

Rawia's blood boiled on recognising who the masked stranger was. She turned away from the window scalded, determined not to let Arwa steal her years of yearning and hard work so easily. Venomous and blazing in a crackling smoke, she threw herself onto the bed to put out the flames ravaging her from within.

Arwa was tired the next morning. Still recovering from the nightly venture, she had eaten most of the kunafah[2] in the platter without realising it. Her mind ate for her, it was doing over-time. Her core drive within steered her to feed her growing relationship. But, it was slowly draining her out mentally and physically to the point where her daily chores were difficult to complete. She became absorbed in thinking about their future exotic encounters, and how the thrill of self-restraint was becoming increasingly strenuous on them both. It had occurred to them to put off their visits until marriage, but they found their minds pleading for the pleasure of each another's company all the more. Soul coveted soul in a roaring fever. Their self inflicted limits backfired. Communication of some sort had to be maintained, it was decided. Everything in moderation was wise. But was it possible to put a quota on love?

She peered long and hard into the open courtyard. It was a cool morning, the desert winds still tumultuous, slackening a little at well spaced intervals. Her eyes captured a pleasing sight on the boundary wall: a group of Agamid lizards socialised. Their flaming red and deepening purple scaly skins collaged, transfusing a force of nature into the palace. He found his family, Arwa noticed, then turned away hunching in emotion. The question troubling her still lingered: when would she meet the two remaining members of her own family? Were they even alive? She would ask Atif to carry out a search for them one day.

Bending down to finish the laced skirt beadwork on her dress, she smiled furtively to herself, imagining Atif's reaction when she would clothe herself like a shiny pearl before him. She secured the last bead at the hem of the layered skirt, and stepped back to marvel her creation. There was no doubt, the laced gown was exquisitely appealing to the eye. She had left the sleeves without the silk lining so that the lace imprint would adorn her skin with flowery patterns, and the low cut bodice was moulded to precision against her own curves. Tonight, she would be the one surprising him.

Whilst the palace slept, caught in a tangle of sheets, Arwa stood enchanted by her appearance in the mirror. A tall, single candle lit the room. Skirts radiated out from her waist like petals from the throat of a rose, she noticed a change – not a soft, subtle one, but a substantial one. It peeked at her from behind her shoulders. It was the fact that she was *wanted*. Her facial expression painted the change, the pouted lips, the permanent rouge in her cheeks from hours of blushing, even her eyes captured a jewel-like intensity, similar to that of the crown on her head. Repetitively she had pinned her hopes in the distance. And then the pins just fell out, loosely pushing themselves from their holes. Presently her expectations were near, and she was close enough, confident enough to reach out to them.

The flame quivered. Its shadow shivered.

The evening spread its wings over the undulating architecture of the palace. After Maghrib prayer, the dull muteness which usually gagged the palace was interrupted by the sound of the troops returning from their back-breaking preparations. Murad led the march, standing proudly and taut with the new weight on his shoulders. It had been a trying task for them all, but determination ensured that they had succeeded. Excelled, in *his* personal case. He unconsciously touched the blue turban on his head which pronounced him Sergeant Major.

He released the men for a deserving break, and rushed to show Arwa his Shield of Merit. Every sweat droplet, every strained muscle was worth the recognition he had received from his seniors. He wondered how she would react to the achievement. Would she even react? He reminded himself not to get too carried away. As he approached the corridor where her room was situated, he calmed his pace into a manly stature. He did not want to appear excessively eager. To his dismay, the door was wedged by a strip of wood curling off from the frame. He debated on whether to peer inside, but he found that he could not resist.

Inside, Arwa was dressed like a soft dove adorned with a white splash of beads around her. She resembled a white musk flower, delicate and elegantly shaped to perfection. Her locks were piled on top of her head into definitive rolls, revealing the deep cut of the bodice until the beginning of her waist. Her palms were decorated with shapes drawn carefully in henna.

Murad's blood stewed in ecstasy. Was she really making such an effort for his return? He had expected praise, but this truly exceeded his expectations. She raised her hand to put on the kohl to intensify her lustrous appeal. Murad noticed the silver handcuff on her wrist, as she carefully outlined her lower eyelids. He wondered if he should intrude on her surprise for him. Before he turned away, he took one last look to satisfy his appetite at her preparing herself for him.

Arwa removed the handcuff and replaced it with an expensive, gaudy gold bracelet. Next, she put on an equally if not more precious ornament on her head. His heart tightened and tugged knotted chains. Crack.

The spangle of stars that he had expected to brighten the evening plunged, one by one, to the ground. She did not love him. She was the light of someone else's happiness. Unable to withstand the magnitude of the shock, two rounded tears rolled down each of his cheeks. Wiping them with the sleeve which held his shield, he made his way back to his room, injured and bleeding with each foot print he made out of his illusion.

With inward satisfaction, Arwa twirled in front of the tiny mirror. A pure replenished symbol of fertility, her reflection resembled the slim youthful figure of a celestial dancer. She could almost see herself floating in a chariot with Atif, far into the ceremonial courts of their wedding. Since it was almost time for her to depart to the well, she covered herself with the black veil and pierced out into the darkness like a delighted glow worm.

Arwa awaited Atif's arrival. She kicked the green earth clumping at the edge of the well impatiently. They chose the well because it *was* public, so that they could pretend that they had come for water if someone caught them. Exhausted by time, she resolved to visit his bedroom. Perhaps he was in pain, or Sheikh Khalil's health could have deteriorated further. To flee from her own rambling perceptions, she turned the dazzling waters of the night in the sheikh's direction.

She headed towards Atif's sleeping quarters, passing a gallery of thick cream alcoves, each lit with blue lanterns on the way. They shed a ghostly, unblinking light upon the paintings on the walls that shrunk away from their templates of realism. The curves, the dimensions, the spherical intensity flattened out into the wall itself. The heavily jewelled light-pulls hovered aimlessly as Arwa swerved past.

An excited expression brushed across her face as she drew nearer to the lacquered entrance of his bedroom. She caught sight of her reflection in one of the geometric mirrored mosaics encrusted into the marble walls. Her appearance was shabby, the purdah increasingly worn out by the sandy, salty winds whipping it ferociously in the night time. But never mind, she consoled herself, the illuminating glow of the pearl he would witness tonight would blow him away into a foreign land.

A faint female trill echoed in the hallway outside his bedroom door. Arwa went closer to find out what was happening. The door was slightly ajar. It revealed the complaisant tone of the atmosphere inside. Few candles created beckoning shadows of the bulky furniture. The voice became louder, humming softly to itself. The stone flowers in the door to his room stirred. She felt the henna orchestra of geometry slice into her palms. The giant rose pool beside his bed beckoned mockingly. Sugary almond cookies were arranged neatly in a circular silver tray. Two single cups sent a thousand reflections meditating out of the door.

Arwa felt an icicle of distrust pierce her spine. What was

this? She pushed open the door in a single, powerful movement. The tears in her eyes seared into her heart. The stampede of the vision flattened her.

The naked backs of the pair were visible.

The fabric screeched painfully against Arwa's burning skin.

There lay Atif, draped across his bed, peacefully asleep in the lap of a female who stroked his hair. His oiled skin beckoned lasciviously. The lady dazily continued humming as if she was hypnotised. They were congealed, affixed like gum.

Arwa made her escape, the thorns of agony shredding her thriving heart.

The chariot whisked away without her.

---

[1] Lawful under Islamic law

[2] Vermicelli pudding

Chapter 19

The sun washed its red face.

Khalil turned his face towards the mirror. Was it the face of a charismatic, dependable father? Or was it the face of a treacherous, conniving brother? Calmly casual, that was Khalil's style. He acted as if he hadn't murdered his brothers, as if he hadn't slaughtered his courtesans. Quick casualties that soon died. He was as dangerous as he was kind. As angry as he was soft. Moral as he was immoral. In reality, there was really only one thing to hate about him: his two faces. Confused between the two masks his eyes witnessed, his ducts squirted a rope of slimy grey tears.

But who was to blame? His mother. Females were always the ignition to a man's sins; their fragile femininity was a façade, a cloak on their more sly personalities. His mother had forced him to murder his step-brothers, to keep the coffee throne, the trade empire solely for himself. He was only fifteen when she cajoled him into trampling his lineage. No amount of reluctance, whether cries, weeping or stubbornness worked their power upon her. She was as brutal as a man in a woman's body. She threatened to burn him. His mother was a stout swarthy woman, possessing an incredible ferocity in her temper. He never understood what comfort his father found in her except for her youth.

Chilly beads of sweat slithered down his face.

'Mama, Mama, I don't want to kill them, I can't!' The child-boy cried, echoes capturing an unpleasant memory. She didn't care for any bond. The only relationship which mattered to her was that of power. And this power could take any form, through strength, wealth, title or reputation. At any cost, she ensured Khalil usurped all four.

A faint burn journeyed roughly up his spine until it eventually struck the epicentre of his skull. 'Allah forgive me! Allah forgive me!' he whispered, gulping the foam ball that was enlarging in his throat. Bats flitted in the cave where he had disposed of the bodies. Vultures tore away bone from flesh. The burnings of the soles of his feet continued until he had murdered all three of his younger brothers. His mother said he was a true man, and gratified him with gold. Childhood was meant to be spent as a free spirit, dreaming of the future. As soon as he passed puberty, Khalil obtained ownership to three spirits and a future. He wanted the same for Atif. That's what his mother had made him believe: Khalil was a scavenger supporting his pure race. When concubines became pregnant, he killed them to restore a promising future for Atif, who was the *only* son he wanted. He would never let Atif go through the terror of killing his own sibling. He did the deed for him.

Khalil stared long and hard into the mirror again, the odour of murder panting straight at him. Clumps of moulted dust balls protruded from his face in snowy tufts. The corrugated skin surrounding his eyes barely supported the weight of his decaying eyeballs. His ears were unsymmetrical and jagged, sticking out of his head like two leaves flapping on a lonely branch. Life was tackling him: Sheikh Khalil was dying.

The fuzzy violet blobs do not belong in Arwa's room. Yet she sees them, dabbing out the other colours in a whirl. Arwa crawled towards the window, dodging her way past the gigantic mutant purple puddles to regain her bearings. Everything was flat, lifeless, just objects. Objects should never hold a meaning for any-one. It was better this way.

She felt her heart melt, drop by drop, thickening her blood with misused emotion. Her soul burst apart like the roasted skin of a chestnut; the shell of which split. A multiplier effect of de-struction. The new split then further divorced itself from its previ-ous partner. Helpless at the prospects of her illusive Fate, she col-lected her final tear with her fingertip and watched it absorb into the saturated cloth. How could she have been attracted astray like that? Especially since Atif's father was a womaniser and she had had that knowledge! As the facts asserted themselves profoundly together, she found her heart swarming deeper into a bottomless pit.

Arwa sobbed bitterly. Her heart was captured only to be hurled back into the mouth of a black ocean. It seemed as if she had to shuffle further along to the peak of a climax of which she had no sense of navigation. Where was she supposed to go? Who was she fooling? Or rather, who was fooling her? The Love Spook. This was the beginning and this was the end.

Too confused to decide how to react, she felt the best op-tion for her would be to leave the palace once and for all. If she stayed, memories of the enchanting excursions and the twinkling nights would only cause her a further river of pain. She gathered her belongings and placed them into the centre of the room. Yes, self-banishment was the safest option.

Murad stuck his head out of the window and analysed each side. The bodies he discovered in the mountains played on his mind. His heart was doing its nervous dance all over and would not allow him to sleep. The issue was not that Murad was un-safe, but he could be endangered any second. He wished that he had never been adopted. Khalil had always treated him like a son, providing all the care and concern. But the fact still was that Khalil was not his true father, and he could never truly trust him. A bird hooted above his window. He jumped. There was no point in staying any longer. He would live longer and happier if he had a new working environment. Perhaps he would return after Sheikh Khalil had passed away.

Her presence didn't budge from its place in his heart. Although Murad was aware that confronting Arwa would only uproot his rejected feelings, he felt he had to let her know exactly what she was putting aside – and for whom! He had deduced the previous evening that such expensive items could be only gifted by an aristocrat, and the only aristocrat around Arwa was Atif. Countless nights he had spent, lulling himself into an empty fantasy, diving further and further into an ocean of dishonesty. He was most hurt by the fact that he was able to compete for her affections. Sheikh Atif was everything he was not: wealthy, educated and an aristocrat. Ready to shed what shadowed his broken heart, he carried himself like a male bull, his chin tucked into his chest and his horns ready to attack. Shoulders jutting forward, he hunted for her room. He thumped Arwa's door.

She didn't open it.

He knocked again, only this time the thuds were louder.

No response.

Unable to control the turmoil riding vigorously through him, he hurled it open. The area was sectioned, the outskirts were bare, and all traces of life were removed and piled into a heap in the core. Only the white dress and the golden jewellery lay sprawled all over the bed.

The door to the hammam[1] opened quietly Arwa entered, looking pale and blue like a ghoul.

Shivers crawled up his spine, mollifying the gales that had spewed in with her entrance. 'Where are your going?'

'I'm leaving the palace. Forever.'

Dismayed at the sudden turn in events, Murad asked the cause of her sudden departure.

'I have been lead on into a tangled situation, from which I want to release myself once and for all. The only vent out of this suffocation is for me to leave.' She bundled up the clothes on the floor.

Somewhat refreshed that the relationship between her and Sheikh had collapsed, he inquired where she intended to depart to.

She didn't answer straightaway, as if deeply absorbed in thinking about the appropriate response. She told him that she was going to sail away from the port of Aden to a new place, to an improved peace, a fresh beginning.

'Arwa, I want to come with you.'

'With me?'

'Yes.'

'What will you do with a broken heart. What *can* you do with a broken heart? It has been used and abused too many times. You have a future here,' she reminded him, not giving much attention to what he was offering her. Murad was offering *himself* to her.

'You may feel that you are the one with the broken heart. I almost broke mine too,' he said, grateful that he had arrived in time to catch her.

She was too busy arranging her belongings and securing them with twine to notice.

He decided to wait to disclose his offering in full until they reached their destination. A tranquillity descended on him, pouring his empty heart with hope.

'Arwa wait, I will not allow you to travel un-chaperoned.'

'I am used to my solitude. Please do not intrude.'

'My intention is not to intrude. Wounds take time to heal. For a moment we wander in silence, the nearer things seeming further away than the distant ones. But in reality the further things are more permanent.' he said, his eyes focused on the floor.

Arwa was enticed by truth in his words, but they only pricked further into her cuts. 'It would have been better if you hadn't said anything at all.' She didn't want to get involved or commit to anything right now. Calmly however, she picked up a pattern book and began to flip through it, wondering the extent to which she would have to engage in conversation with him.

'You are right.' He looked directly into her watery eyes, 'But Arwa, there is still one sentence I have not yet said, maybe because Fate did not grant me the permission. One day you will see that my constancy towards you will be recompensed.' He left the room to prepare to accompany her on their new birth together.

It was evening time. Atif looked out of the window, yawning out of his sleep. Slowly standing up, he wondered why he had slept so deeply. He scratched his chest to find that it was damp with rose water. What *had* happened the night before? He knew he had missed his episode with Arwa. All he could recall was that he drank his afternoon mint tea and intended to pay a short visit to Abati before praying for him in the mosque. Later his eyes would devour the company of sweet Arwa.

He had missed the Asir congregation, so he decided to pray in his room. For the past few days he had been increasingly emotionally dispensed, with the shrinking moments with his father and the flourishing intimacies with Arwa. Both experiences were opposites, one compensated the other. After he had completed the prayer, he decided to visit Arwa first to apologise for his absence the night before, the rest of the night he would spend with Abati.

He walked past his servants in the direction of her room and felt their stares poking him in his back. Opening the door to her deserted room, he saw the white dress and his presents left purposely on the bed. Nothing else, not a trace of a presence was anywhere. A wisp of delusion entered and capered around the bed.

She left.

She abandoned him at a time when he most needed her, when his father was struggling for survival on his death bed. He reached for the dress. He screamed and shouted to his servants for immediate service. 'Does anyone know where Arwa is?'

Silence.

'I do sir,' said a small black boy. 'She left after Asli for the port of Aden.'

'Aden?'.

'Yes.' said the boy. 'She was very distressed. She told me to say farewell to Rawia because she was running out of time. Then she left with Sergeant Major Murad.'

Sergeant Major Murad? What was going on? 'Order the doorman to prepare my stallion. I'm going to look for her.'

The galloping wild horse coasted towards the canoes bobbing on the shore. He tried to catch sight of her. Atif wondered what had reduced their colourful forest into a colony of weeds. The more he thought about it, the further his nerves crispened. He heard them crunch in his chest. A breeze blew his head scarf into his face. As he pushed it aside, he saw Arwa standing on the platform of the Jeddah ships waiting beside the dock pole. 'Alhumdullilah,' he said in his head, as he rushed towards her.

'Arwa,' he cried, 'Arwa!' He knew she had heard him and was deliberately looking away. Stepping onto the platform, he pulled her towards him. 'Where are you going?' His expression so stiff that it seemed his face would crack.

She pulled back her arm with matching strength. 'Far away from your lies and deceits.' She defended her decision vehemently, with the force of the despair that obstructed her.

'Lies and deceits! What are you saying?'

'Do not pretend you do not know. Innocence does not suit the wicked. I am hurt that my life dangles on cheap affections. Go away Atif, for both our sakes.'

He backed off. 'How could you leave me? I have played blissfully and faithfully in love with you, and you feel you can just detach yourself from me.'

Arwa wanted to slap him so hard that his body would rattle. 'That is precisely what you have done. Played. And you continue playing.' She turned to walk away.

'Wait! What is this evilness that lurks in your head. What have I done to deserve your accusations?' He took a firm grasp of her shoulders.

'I came last night to your bedroom. I saw you lying in her embrace. My heart was shattered.' She tried to wriggle out of his grip. 'Now let me leave.'

'You must have dreamt it,' said Atif, deeply agitated at the magnitude of accusations she was making. He was dashed by her unaccommodating assertiveness.

'I know what I saw.'

'But it is not true. I must have been drugged. I only love you.'

'Eyes do not deceive.' She almost leapt out of her own shadow to find Murad who had gone to load their luggage.

'Just because I am older than you does not mean that I have any experience. I am equally as innocent as you are.' Atif shouted after her, the blustery wind scraping her hair into his face.

'Prove it!'

Overcome with agitation, he ran after her. To escape his domineering presence she stepped onto a small boat. He jumped into the boat with her, sending her flying onto the wet floor. With one arm he pulled her up and looked into her eyes. They looked away. He thrust his mouth upon her, capturing her lips in a passionate assault. His other hand held hers lacing between her fingers and tightening, he pushed in his tongue further. She tried to pull away, but he buried his hand into the thickness of her hair and urged her mouth into his. His body clung to hers, the waves spraying water all over them in the small boat. She felt her bosom crush against his rigid chest and fell captive to his tight embrace. Their bodies coiled into a warm nectar, despite the cold water splashing upon them. Pressing her against the wood, his tongue dipped further into her mouth and they absorbed into one another. It was a long, stimulating kiss. He devoured her with pleasure.

He pulled away to catch a breath. 'There, do you think I have ever done that before?' He suddenly realised the pairs of eyes focusing upon them from all around.

Recovering from the sudden withdrawal of the magnetism of his mouth, Arwa stood up. It was clear that it was his first kiss. She did not know how she knew, but she knew. She knew he felt what she felt.

'I will follow,' she said. 'But, I must tell Murad.'

Atif left. His damp clothes outlined the muscular form that his robes modestly covered. He knew that she would follow. He didn't need to think twice.

She waved back at him in approval.

Arwa found Murad loading the luggage at the back of the ship. 'Murad, I've changed my mind,' she said, 'Let's stay, it will be better for the both of us.'

He battled in his head with what had brought about the change. He unwillingly unloaded their belongings without a question. The prospect of a struggle didn't bother him, but the situation did. He knew that her trust had been pricked once, and he was wise enough to know that if something happened once, it would inevitably happen again.

---

[1] Bathroom

Twisting the Tale

'All daughters are princesses.' Andrew told her that. For once, he was right.

The sky resembled multicoloured drops of rippled silk: blue, lilac and bronze curved and curled clouds swifted through the cool air in friendly batches. The blue and lilac tufts of thick cotton formed a team above the lonely golden bronze mesh balls, bobbing against the boundary of the white silken hills in the distance. A magnificent fountain sprayed the horizon with diamond droplets, each drop completing its silvery trail in the synchronised swim. Salsabil. Sweet chilly dribbles on a hot summers day. Two clear blue transparent rivers sliding over beds of glossy pearls ran their course side by side. Like twins. One tasted of fizzy flower nectar, and the other was as succulent and syrupy as honey.

Along the azure riverbanks stood beautifully painted trees resembling feminine contours like archways over the track of the symphony of streams. Pinks, purples, reds, yellows, oranges - a rainbow procession of petals swayed elegantly in the tasteful breeze. Fruits in contrasting colours to the petals shook on silent waves of air. The ripe ones knew who they were and floated down slowly to satisfy eager people's desires, served on shiny silver trays.

Young children carrying trays and goblets inlaid with gems served the honoured people. Gifts of gold embedded in the exhilarating gardens caused the delighted expressions of many to glow with gratitude. In the distance she saw a healthy young Helena, able to devour the precious moments with her children, without being frightened of infecting them or making herself weak. Daud's clone in all ages played around her. Girls who resembled her, shared laughter under the same umbrella. Arwa guessed that they were children who had been born dead. It took her a few moments to recover from the paragon of perfection that drove her eyes in all directions.

But she was yet to be amazed.

She turned around to see the sight behind her, and she was presented with two keys by a young page. The first key was liquid silver, shining calmly in her palm resembling mercury. The second key was golden, much heavier than the first and glamorously inlaid with emeralds along its spine.

A few pearl-faced transparent ladies floated by, their golden hair trailing behind them like royal cloaks. They were going to one of two places: the sparkling ruby palace, chiselled intricately to reveal the silver towers, windows and silver gateways or the gleaming green castle lined with doors of gold that glowed with a blinding force.

The keys remained in each one of her hands. She was expected to make a choice. Slowly and steadily she floated on the bouncy lush green grass towards the boundary wall between the two captivating citadels. Outside each gate was a box. Carefully they were uplifted by an invisible force towards her and the lids were flipped to bare the contents.

So this was the decision she had to make. A Choice for Eternity.

The decision didn't take much time. She took the box she favoured and entered the high structured building. The floor was coloured but clear, revealing the purities of its construction. It gleamed with the flickers of light from the crystal flower droplets on the chandeliers that hung on the elevated ceiling. A silken carpet rolled out automatically beneath her feet, leading her to the lock which would fit the key.

A festival of rose scented fragrance greeted her as she turned the key. The room was a treasure of tranquillity. Soft feathery cushions in fabrics never seen before by man swarmed around the bed. The bed was a towering pulpit, encrusted with topaz jewels and quilts, heavily embroidered with silken accuracy. A closer look at the bed revealed that it was not covered with topaz shaded fabric. In actual fact, the quilt was slippery sheets of spring water, lukewarm, sliding over one another in layers. Water held its shape without a vessel.

She caught her reflection on one of the pillows. She looked very different. Her skin was clear, almost transparent and spread delicately over her structure. A tirade of dark curls stole over her shoulders in a shawl. Glassy brown eyes were outlined with long, thick lashes that were spangled with twirling stars.

There was no doubt about it. The glory of the after-life was infinite.

Casting her eyes around the room, she searched for him. Where was he? He appeared before her, bursting with youth in a thick velvet cloak. Taking sailing strides towards her, he held out a perfectly carved hand in her direction. She accepted. She allowed him to pull her into his embrace. For a while, they just remained fixated in the other's gaze, reading the surprised emotions which bound them together.

Her skin rolled in response to his touch. So close. So warm. So tingly. She put her arms around his thick broad shoulders, letting the cloak slide off. An adoring desire quaked within her chest as he appeared in nothing but in his strong, sturdy form before her. They stood like reflections falling in a sea of sensation, before he picked her up and threw her onto the bed. The aqua quilts splashed, but did not make them wet.

He towered over her, gently placing his mouth over hers, the softness enticing her to part her lips wider. His large beckoning tongue seared into the opening, rolling hotly with her on the bed of pumping passion. It was a long, lingering kiss, with neither participant pausing for a breath. As their bodies met, mingled feelings of discovery and pleasure pulled them in further. Skin greeted skin, backing away at first with surprise, then locking itself with welcome.

He felt her breast press against his chest under him, the nipples teasing the hairs as he rocked above her in the mounting kiss. Slowly, and carefully, he unwrapped her from the smooth robe draped over her. Her hands clung to his hair as she felt the fabric sliding away from her. The intensity of the exposed ecstasy caught them both. He pulled away from the absorbing waves of her mouth as she moaned with pleasure at the sight of him.

Every muscle was expertly crafted, placed in perfection liken an artist's sculpture.

Every curve was carefully tapering and twisting like the subject of a painting.

She stroked his bulging biceps to reassure herself that he was real.

He plucked her nipples to confirm they would react.

They did.

He drank from the bowls of her bosom, flicking his tongue feverishly over the peaks whilst his hands stroked her thrumming navel. The mounting pleasure urged them both to discover the depths of their pressing needs. Question after question was answered with an intimate invitation.

Hot and demanding, his body rolled over impatiently as

she climbed on top of him. Nuzzling into his neck, she sucked on the delicate flesh of his ears. As if surprised that such a powerful physique was capable of having such a tender piece attached to it, she gazed into his face, telling him of her bursting urge.

The army of nerves prepared for the assault.

Lifting himself on top of her once again, he pressed his lips against her, lowering himself in steps so as not to hurt her. She shuddered with ripping delight. Caressing her navel, he eased himself into the blushing pink fold spread out in front of him. The opening gulped it in slow, slender swallows.

Their bodies yearned for one another as he ventured in, breaking the seal to the explosion laying await inside. She could feel him inside of her, as if he was a part of her own body. Locked into the steamy cave of each others bodies, musky sweat beads arranged themselves neatly in a pattern on their skin. He pushed, lusting in love. He wanted to reach the very core of her. She held him tightly within her, letting him explore her to fulfilment.

The rocking went on for what seemed days.

They sailed on merging waters for decades.

She was aboard the Dreamboat.

Warm, scented bubbling water splashed onto them, purifying them for the next session.

'Here,' she said, handing him the box.

He opened it and took out the jewellery. He placed it on her wrist.

The silver handcuff adorned her naked form. They both paused and stared at it for a little while, breathless. The stone was a real ruby this time.

'Shukran Arwa. Shukran,' he said eventually, turning himself on top of her again.

The ruby red dreamboat glided away into bliss.

Chapter 20

The well was a public resort, and the lovers found that it was not a safe place to meet for long. Sheikh Khalil's health continued to scratch itself out, so they agreed to meet after he recovered, after a week. As their mutual attachment tightened, suspicions against them deepened. Atif's root to power was foreseen by the viziers and he was lost in a political frenzy of formalities. Pressure mounted on him so much that the appointment he had made with Arwa slipped into a crack in the heaping responsibilities.

When they had returned to the palace Arwa was given all sorts of tasks to do, chores which she had never attempted previously (such as polishing the silverware and washing the drapes) occurring to a shortage of staff. Everyday she dreamt of how she would be released from the labour and become the mistress of the palace. Her chafed palms and tired legs worked hard, in anticipation of the awe inspiring thrill at the end of the week. She decided she would dress up again in the white dress and the emerald jewellery he had given her. In her longing for his company she wrote verses, long curvy sentences of their intoxicating thirst for one another. She rolled up the scroll and left it on her dresser.

On the night of their appointment, Arwa limped lazily into her room. Her feet were sore from stretching and hanging the drapes all day. Nevertheless, an excitement invigorated her. She quaked at the prospect of meeting Atif again. She wondered how they would react since their last encounter had been so intimate. She firmly warned herself that she would remain cool to his advances, as she rummaged through the closet to find the gown and jewellery. They would both have to wait patiently until they were lawful for one another. She did not want to appear frigid, but recalling how easily she was whipped into a steamy storm in the boat, she needed to build up her will power. Instructions of self-restraint were chanted in her head. God consciousness was not a characteristic many people had, and she felt that if she mastered it she would be rewarded.

The outfit and accessories were absent. She scrambled deeper into the shelves, searching frantically for the items. They were not there. Perhaps Rawia would know where they were. Solutions grew out of her like magic. Treading quietly down the hallway, so as not to meet the suspicion drenched eyes of the other servants, she wondered if the items could have been stolen. May Allah forbid, she thought shuddering, Atif would never forgive her.

Unfortunately, Rawia's door was locked. She'd have to ask her tomorrow then. Arwa turned away. A shattering mirror crashed loudly behind the door. She spun around and looked through the keyhole to check that Rawia was alright. A stubby candle gasped by the wavering drapes at Rawia's balcony window.

The shadow of her rounded figure leaned out over the balcony awkwardly. It did not move. An abhorrent feeling of worry and annoyance spooked Arwa. What on earth was Rawia doing? She decided to break the lock open. The nearest item around was a torch lighter. She picked up the rusted pole and thrust it deep into the hole. She shook it until it finally unlatched.

The door swang open, banging into that wall.

Arwa ran to the balcony. 'Rawia! Rawia! What is happening?' She pulled the woman off from the rail and onto the floor. To her horror, her blue dress was stained with red. 'Are you alright?'

Her drowsy, pink eyes looked up into Arwa's face. 'Arwa! Arwa! You must escape,' she said in between breaths. 'Atif will kill you, he has gone mad.' She heaved in deeply. 'He did this to me. He did this to prove to his father he was not impotent, that their trade empire would survive no matter what.' Her head flopped onto one shoulder.

Arwa held Rawia in her arms, trembling with fright. Rawia was her mother, her friend, her everything. She was the only one endowed with an expansive heart towards her from the beginning. Rawia's love for the three little girls was incomparable. She wanted to evade the reality emerging deliberately before her, but she could not.

'Rawia, why, why would he do this?'

'He tried to kill me!' She gasped to catch a breath. 'If my words mean anything to you, leave my child. Escape from this treacherous man, he is just like his father. It is only because of the Sergeant Major Murad that I fled from his ravaging rage.' Sweat streamed down her face in rivulets. 'He took and sabotaged the core of my womanhood. He will repeat his heinous acts until he can face the last taunts of his father. Elope Arwa! Elope with Murad, he is a much better person. Elope!'

The stench of betrayal, fluorescent and acidic, leaked into the room. Her face turned pale, weak, sickening. Arwa aroused herself from the doom that trapped. *Why* would Atif do this? Was he really that mad? Her soul pleaded to be told otherwise.

She bent towards Rawia. 'Rawia you must tell me the truth.'

'I promise I am telling you what is better for you, leave! Leave!' Rawia cried, flailing her arms in the air like a vulture. 'He even made me put on a white dress and this jewellery before he penetrated me. After he was finished he ripped the items off, saying that he would need them for his next bride!'

Arwa's heart choked. Rawia's knifey words made it splutter. Was it not mandatory for him to be faithful to her? She recalled him saying, 'There are things that you do not know about me, and I do not know about you. It is actually better this way.' What ever did he mean? Wasn't transparency what he always preached? In a way, he had the capacity to be vicious. A viciousness that vexed her. It all made sense. The items had been *taken* from her room. Stolen for his theatrical fantasies! Both father and son were crazy.

'Rawia will you be alright? I am not leaving you like this.'

'I was born, have lived and I will die here. This is my home. Don't you worry about me, I shall be fine. I must warn the other girls in the palace, but his next victim is you,' the panting woman assured her. 'My blessings are with you, my dear.' She smiled wearily from pain. 'Leave!'

Arwa clutched her for the last time. She debated a plan of action. Her soul ripped apart as she fled to her room to repeat her evacuation. Only this time, it was for real. Stones hammered upon her, harder than before.

The trees guarded the white body of the palace. The winds arched the white sands that brewed around the palace, slapping it sombrely. She trudged heavily out of the net that tried to haul her back in. She was a small silvery fish amongst others that would also be swimming in a whirlpool of spume. She worried about her companions. She stooped outside the palace gates. The vision of her dream castle crumbled into a pile of decay. The once impressive accumulation of towers was nothing but a yellowing, rocky lump.

She yelled at the top of her destitute throat: 'I hope you never live in a moment of peace, Atif. I hope you are betrayed as badly as you have deceived me!'

She wept with rage.

She grieved for herself.

The powdery orange mist lifted the caravan and trailed un-swervingly behind her.

'Jazak Allahkhair,' whispered Khalil. Atif offered him some more water. Khalil raised his withering grey eyelids to stare at his aging son. He was a man of firm determination, noble-souled and granted with an expansive aptitude for ruling. Yet, it troubled the crumbling Sheikh that his son was not settled. Atif was emotional; proven to be lead by heart rather than his head which diluted his virility. Yet, a recent glow spread across his face at times, sugges-tive of paradise transplanted, and calmed Khalil's aspirations for him. Perhaps he would die relieved after all.

'Atif, my son, time is short and I will be leaving soon.' He reflected on the effect of his own words. It was true; he was dying right before his son. 'Atif do not indulge in the worldly pleasures which I have wrapped myself in, they are a debt that must be re-paid. The next world I am leaving for will demand the payment and I am afraid I have no savings to support me there.' His back stiffened like the trunk of a palm tree.

With blood streaked eyes, stinging from the last hours of duty he was spending with his father, Atif glared at him. 'Are you referring to the death of my mother and the murder of my sister?' The words escaped his mouth before he could control them.

'What are you talking about?' Khalil's his voice quivered. His face crumpled into a singular frown.

Blood thundered through his veins in a flood. How could this man even deny his sins on his death bed? His ribs almost cracked with anger. 'For goodness sake Abati, for once release the megalomania to which you forcefully hold yourself captive. You will find ease.' The words were spat out.

'I am not a device, or an animal driven by lust, I am actually in great agony.' Then he changed his tone. 'Isn't there a little bit of power which we all crave for? Aren't we all victims to it?'

'No Abati, that's what you have taught yourself.'

'Hah!' Khalil barked, his mouth agape like a dog waiting for meat to be thrown into it. 'We all must surrender to megalomania, you understand? It's an addiction. There will come a point in your life when, you have no choice but to follow its lead. No one can escape its temptation. Death is one exit out, preoccupying yourself with other sins is another.' He gasped for breath.

'The poor are not victims to it.'

'Oh no Atif, that is where your naivety worries me, of course the poor are! Power is a system that lurks in society, beggars must pay fees to the head man, eunuchs must pay half their earnings to their pimps…I think I have sheltered you too much–'

'Eunuchs! But they are born that way!'

Khalil guffawed at him. 'No one is born castrated, the pimps castrate them when they are very young to earn money for them. I have a special place for them in my heart, so I have hired them throughout the palace.'

'What a great deed you have done Abati.'

Khalil appealed to the sky. His eyes sailed heavenward. 'These small things might balance my scales for the day. Son, never forget about your scales like I have, they should be your top priority.' He blinked his singed eyelids. Watching the fury wrap itself onto his son's skin, Khalil realised that his son was aware of the tragedy that had been inflicted into their home decades ago. 'Atif, Atif look at me.' He waited for a response. Atif looked at him, his eyes flashing fiercely. 'I do not know for how long you have come to know about this or who told you—'

'I have known since the day it happened! I was the only witness to the incidents Abati.'

'My son!' Khalil cried, tears blurring his vision. 'I am sorry you got to know, I only wanted to protect you from the scandal.'

'The scandal? What scandal?'

'Your mother was a gentle woman, but extremely emotional. I had to treat her like a child, constantly entertaining her surging energy with new toys, jewels, trips and banquets.' He recalled her innocent memories. 'Often I would leave for business trips and she would be left alone for days, sometimes even weeks. She complained of being neglected and the effect it was having upon her health. Then came a year when there was tremendous fall in the mocha crops, prices surged upwards and the demand fell immensely, all the coffee traders were in hardship. At this time I increasingly left home to stabilize the economy of the western region. I appointed a Hakim, by recommendation, to treat you mother.' The water goblet slipped from his hand. The undrunk water splashed into a splatter of elongated puddles on the tiled floor.

'Go on.'

'My father stimulated my spirit,' Khalil said. 'My mother thieved my soul. I wanted to protect you from the thorns that I was forced to endure. I bled and I bled, but I did not let as much as a splinter ever come and prick you. The Hakim betrayed me, he bewitched your mother and they committed adultery.' He screamed. 'Oh Allah, why did my son live with such a burden on his chest! Why!' His head fell back onto the pillow, his stretched nerves loosened. He made a short, final gasp.

Life ebbing from his face. At the surface of the mask, the two-sided mirror eyes jutted out, and then quickly back in again:

the cargo of mercy sailed away. 'Lailaha Illallah Muhammad Ur rasul allah,' With these last whispers his jaw dropped and his heart was extracted. Expired, the container of his soul lay bleached and lifeless before his gaping son, tossing and tortured in the flash of events without a movement.

'Abati! Abati! Forgive me!' Atif sobbed, feeling his heart wringing itself all over his father's dead body. Actuality and mis-interpretations collided with one another. Sparks of repugnance showered the death bed. He carried his bleeding heart dripping to the servants in the room.

'Prepare for the funeral.' His voice was barely audible.

The men understood and nodded to confirm the sentence. Rocky stones weighed down his throbbing head. Atif decided he needed to be relieved from the pain and anguish being hurled towards him. He was the last person! The last person in the Ali dynasty. The sole existence. He had clung to his father's meta-phorical presence so long that this independence troubled him. Arwa would understand. She would soothe the uncomfortable heat that scorched him. He staggered towards her room, but fell in the middle of the hallway.

Zealous footsteps hurried in his direction. 'Sheikh Atif! What are you doing?' The voice resonated along the entire length of the corridor in a belt. It was Rawia.

'I need to meet Arwa!'

Rawia helped him up. She let him walk to the deserted site alone. A blind joy sent a wave through her body. She inwardly celebrated the momentary victory.

Atif entered the room. It was isolated, and carryied a futile stench within the stale air. 'Arwa! ARWA!' He shouted, the vibra-tions sending the mirror screeching to the floor. He caught sight of the scroll that rolled towards his feet. As he bent to pick it up,

Rawia entered. Paranoia plagued his already icy mind.

'Has she left again? What could have happened this time? What had she seen?'

He felt a reassuring hand on his shoulder. 'Sheikh Atif! I would like to inform you that Sergeant Major Murad has resigned. Both him and Arwa eloped last night!' She smiled with pleasure. She handed him the document containing Murad's resignation. His resignation had come at the most appropriate timing.

Atif looked at the outstretched hand containing the scroll. Under her rosy red sleeve, he caught sight of a green, golden glint. He pulled up the sleeve to reveal the bracelet he had given to his beloved. She immediately withdrew her hand.

'How DARE you!' His face blackened with snags of thunder. 'It was you who drugged me the first time! And you were my trustworthy friend.' He slapped her, sending her flying into the hallway. 'Leave! Leave before I sentence you for execution.'

The commotion startled the servants in the building. They rushed to witness their manageress being kicked and thrown out at the hands of Sheikh Atif.

'You treacherous hypocrite! I love her and you made her disappear from my life!' He shook her with as much force as he could. He kicked her. All he knew was that he had been raped of parent and soul mate.

Servants intervened and Rawia managed to escape the abuse. This was not what she had wanted! After years of service what wrong had she done in wanting to satisfy her languished love? His fuming temper pierced her heart. He would never be swayed towards her now. Never.

And it was all her fault.

Chapter 21

Naïve she was. It was confirmed.

Seductive risks she had taken, thinking they were being replaced with trust. Wasn't that supposed to be true love? She had heard that where there was danger, love was buried deep within that fear, like a prison. A Golden Prison. Musk clouds floated in high the room in groups: a symphony of scent.

The musk love drug suffused around her, as she recalled the irresistible pull she had once felt for him. Unconsciously, her heart began pounding in her chest, taking her for a mad dash into the dreamboat. She felt the concoction of their chemicals swirl, synchronising into one another's movements.

With eyes which looked as if they had been soaked in watery porridge, Sheikh Atif entered, followed by a minister and two thin servants. He remained transfixed, rooted to the floor when he saw his beloved sitting on the ottoman piece before him, not knowing what to say. Words tumbled off his tongue. Fettered in the melody swimming in his head, he engaged into the intensity of her presence.

Arwa felt an overwhelming emotion, consuming her from her stomach upwards due to his being there. The insult he had hurled at her jerked itself back into her head and she looked away angrily. Undeniably, they were talking, despite the prying silence wedged in between them. They spoke without words, sentences or sound, the incredible rush of euphoria encircled them, winding them together.

An echo of footsteps got louder as they steered towards their direction.

'Sheikh Atif, Sergeant Major Murad has arrived for the funeral. He is waiting in the camel caravan to be taken into the male compartment,' interrupted a young male voice from the left side of the room.

'See him into the compartment. I will follow,' Atif replied, a spark of chance sprouting in his eyes. He had the uneasy sense that he was trying to cross into a world which he was now alien. Her gorgeous eyes retained their charm, but were now the eyes of a stranger.

The more he stared at her, the further away she wanted to be from him. He did not believe in the sanctity of relationships, in the yoking together of personal disclosures.

How dare he look at her with wounded eyes. She was not going to be a pawn in his theatre any longer! She turned away. Admittedly, it was not easy swivelling away from him, her body felt as if it had to oppose a natural force. It was true, even now, from the distance between them, that she still loved him. She was not going to lie to herself, and that is what made her mad. He didn't really love her. But, she was not going to be a puppet in his forged hypnosis. Not again, and that was final.

Toiling with time, she stood up, erect as a pole and marched to the exit. With each step she felt a sense of hot, strong eagerness filter into her veins. She knew where her future would be beneficial, fertile and most of all, spent happily. Murad was her path to bliss. As she hurried towards her freedom which lay in freshly baked batches outside the palace door, she heard her name being called out.

'Sara! SARA!' The voice pleaded.

Maybe she was imagining things. She continued to walk

towards the camel caravan, which was patiently waiting for her.

'Sara!' the voice beckoned again, urgently.

Arwa froze for a moment. She swept her eyes around to spot the origin of the howling cries. To her amazement, it was Baba. Baba? How did he know her real name?

Murad was sitting isolated inside the camel caravan. Arwa had returned to the palace to unite with Sheikh Atif. There was no space for him now. 'Oh Allah, grant me the strength to deal with my fate. You know what is best for me,' he said, his head falling into his lap. A familiar swishing of sand created by delicate footsteps made him raise his head. Arwa was walking in his direction. In *his* direction, he could not believe it! She wanted him afterall. Murad watched patiently from inside the caravan at his golden luck, when all of a sudden Arwa froze. When she had finally made up her mind, what was this interruption?

Atif swooned after her, studded with love wounds which he wanted to cure. From a distance, he was gushing down the stairs, like a turbulent river ready to flood the meek banks.

A sense of wonder crept gradually over her as Baba limped closer towards her. His skin was beaded with sweat, the beads lodged between the wrinkles of worry engraved into his face. 'Sara, I'm Daud!'

Not believing her ears, she lifted her pounding feet towards the crawling, crippled crusader. A riot of emotions exploded within her with such intensity that she felt them collide with her bones. Crunch.

'Daud, Daud is that really…' Her voice hiccupped in agony.

Baba watched shocked, as her eyes leapt to the sky and flames surrounded her. 'SARA!' he cried, petrified, unable to slow down the rate of events.

She was thrust in the back with a fire lit arrow. It had appeared from nowhere. Blazes of fire flared up on her dress, munching her alive with each voracious flash. She yelled, trying to roll on the floor to put out the flames but the arrow had sunken in too deep. She felt the iron point prickling her heart. She felt herself disappearing. The flames whistled through the air and left livid tears on her body. Each individual flame's tongue licked her with the same viciousness as that of a nightmarish animal, swallowing her in violent gulps. The flames leapt higher, wanting to catch each and every heartbeat. The fire spluttered; it had overeaten.

The three men rushed towards Arwa, trying to tame the scalding monster, before she turned into a lump of coal.. Her cracked skin revealed blackened crusts of blood as they finally managed to extinguish the fire. The head was bald, covered with a few strands of crisp ebony webs. Transformed: she was now a roasted mass of burnt flesh, a human canvas.

Reduced to a burnt mirage in the scorching desert sun.

Phantasmal, she popped into their lives.

A seasonal mirage she popped out, like a shrivelled up blister.

It was as simple as that.

A few days later, the enraged arrow striker was caught scratching messages on the palace walls, squandering beyond the limits of lunacy. She was executed.

Chapter 22

8 Years Later

DREAMBOAT

A dream at innocent tom-boy thirteen,
Showed me, what seemed to be,
A paradise woven with fanatical imagination,
Which I chose not to accept,
It only engendered swarms of affliction:
You did not love me, and I did not love you.

But later on, it proved true;
You looked at me with your deep brown alluring eyes on a holiday,
And proposed, blushing blissfully,
In the twinkling night,
Miraculously moulding my life,
Into what I thought it could never be.

At first my mouth stood agape at the 'ridiculous offer'
We were a loose knot who resolved everyday riddles for each other,
Then I laughed, and acted naturally,
'No,' I replied in my childish manner,
For you deserved better, far better than me,
I was plagued with confusions of grief and joy,
Battling in my head, unsure:
Was the dream divulging into reality?

But you clearly loved me and I knew, somewhere deep inside, I loved you.

It was wrong to think that I was the master of my fate,
For in the future a myriad of your enchanting excursions trailed,
You were reluctant to go back empty-handed each time,
Like an incense stick stripped of its clothing,
Conforming a distinct invitation from God of assurance,
That you were that special chosen one for me,
Which I chose to accept.

I conveyed my feelings when we departed at the port,
Like helpless repelling magnets who were obviously attracted,
For even then I was not convinced,
As I walked away slowly, silently,
I could feel the tender warmth of your eyes gently stroking my back,
Clutching my body with a whirlpool of forces between us,
Gradually enticing me towards you,
While uprooting the feelings hidden away furtively,
Asserting a fresh vision,
I finally turned and looked at you,
Knowing that I had made my decision;
You waved, and I repeated the motion in approval;
You loved me and I loved you.

I waded head-first into an ocean, drowning my-
self into your everlasting protection,
With deep devotion, love letters and mid-
night feasts soon followed every day,
Each action blossoming the new seed of affection,
Embedded within the compassion between us ....
Soon it bloomed into a beautiful breath-taking tree,
With streams of fantasy surrounding it,

And with exotic fruits scattered in a random pat-
tern on the entangling branches;
Sometimes a wind came and blew leaves onto the ground,
More fruit ripened – tastier than the first.

Numbness prevailed when I became posses-
sive in my craziness about you,
I felt shattered, jealous and hurt at the littlest of things,
Our trust grew on a paved path, slowly with time,
Sometimes the previous stones were replaced with new ones,
Completing the route of a healthy relationship,
But I forgot: you loved me and I loved you.

Our bonds tightened for the vasts of eternity,
The love sang out loud in the harmony of two hearts,
Not a day has passed without missing, wanting, or craving you,
Our beauty together was enriching and wonderful,
People blessed us and others wept,
However, our perseverance fuelled our acceptance,
I would go anywhere with you, do anything for you,
For my love was all all I had to give.

Full of an excited spirit of an innocent child,
Let us sail away with one another,
The penultimate reflection we saw in each other,
Which shone crystal-clear: our invaluable fortune,
Touched by the slightest presence of one another,
Whether in presents, voices or memories,
Audaciously provoking passionate desire,
Highlighted with dreams of a wedding day, a house, children;
You loved me and I loved you.

We were to get married when I had ripened,

Two more days of partition, you in your country – I in mine,
Seemed to feel like our hearts were stretched painfully across the globe,
Like tense elastic bands on a board lute,
You were a good listener, a shoulder to lean on,
You were a rare gift, a precious blessing from God,
So the whispers continued and the rendezvous persisted,
Building the foundation of trees within us.

Our hearts throbbed each day,
Our bodies longed for a warm tender breath,
Hopes of magic to sweep us away to meet
one another in a tasteful way,
But glimpses of our treasured moments, jewel by jewel,
Of how we indulged and absorbed into each other,
How an electric shock darted from corner to corner in our bodies,
Tingling the tension of time spent apart,
You madly loved me and I madly loved you.

The sudden explosions of joy when you came to visit,
Bringing comfort and miracles,
Setting our hearts afire with naked crimson flames,
Planning our future, forgetting about what
could, or could not be our destiny,
We marked our naïve and playful intentions with;
The colour of our carpet for the bedroom,
The house we would live in,
Names for our children;
Unfulfilled wishes when you departed,
Which left a painful scar when a storm came
and diluted our speculations,
For everything is fair in love and war?

But yet again we made a mistake – to over-

look that a little sacrifice would pay off later,
The storm was temporary, leaving little changes in its destruction,
Which healed as time passed,
Flourishing hope and trust in God,
For we were meant to be one, not two,
The fissure in us can be mended – not replaced;
With destiny and reality,
So we can exhibit to the world our exemplary love,
Never to be erased, for it was meant to live alive;
You will always love me, and I will always love you.

Solutions will come, sculpting our lives as God pleases,
We would not have encountered for if it was not fate,
Or become so close, so close,
That it would be impossible to break away,
Without leaving a profound suffering of life long misery
He does not like to punish his creations,
But merely tests them with sheer challenges....

You do not walk along side destiny,
Destiny leads you along the way,
Wake me up from my dreamboat,
For He is the Master:
Not I.

His dry, crusting, crumbling fingers rolled up the scroll scrupulously. Every day it was the same routine, he would read her fountain of love for him, yearning desperately that a few drop-lets would revive his crusting soul. But they never did. He was lost in a maze of fury, aimlessly probing for the phenomenon of her creation which had deserted him.

Stranded, he had built a secluded world for himself, with

such elevated walls which soared straight into the sky. No one was admitted an entry. No one was allowed to exit. Not even a simmer of sunlight brightened up any part of the day. It was all exclusive.

Abandoned, he grew to like his loneliness. It grew him up into his present state.

It comforted him in the spring.

It hugged him in the autumn.

They were all the same.

Then one day a miracle occurred. She had stepped out of her grave and was alive again. His prayers were granted! It began with the clinking of anklets echoing through the isolated hallways. Gradually they became louder and louder. Atif was lost, as usual sailing away on the dreamboat, into the depths of his thorny memories.

The footsteps stopped outside his door. Checking her beautifully chiselled face in the dusty sheen of a wall tile, she dared to open the dungeon door. She moved in, with a serpent like grace, a knot of curls stealing down her forehead, her large brown eyes peeking through the gaps. Her teeth glittered like the sun, outlined with a plump piping of rosy lips. The citrus orange outfit clung to her like a second skin, flowing out loosely from the waist downwards.

He felt as if he was transplanted onto her planet. Arwa was back! She was returned. A bevy of ethereal music painted the atmosphere. Lost in the awakening of an extinct sensation, he held out his hand. 'Arwa, will you sail with me this time?'

'Sheikh Atif,' replied the girl, embarrassed by the sudden advance. 'I am not Arwa,' she began, 'She was my sis-,' she said, breaking herself off.

'For me you are a blessing. I cannot believe my Arwa has

reappeared!'

The young girl observed the desperate old man; he was drowning in ancient rivulets of eroded love juice. And anyway, she wanted to settle down as well. Sharp as she was, she looked at the wealth staring back at her.

'Yes, Sheikh Atif,' she said, 'I am your Arwa.'

Arwa's Message

I never imagined that I would be a tourist.

We all have two bodies. I want to talk about the one we only see sometimes, as a reminder of some sort, but rarely ever feel. Striped, polka dotted, floral, tinted or toned, it's up to you what you make of your shadow. Some of us sense it, others are completely unfeeling. Our shadow is our soul.

But it does exist, it will spring into animation as soon as its representation time is over.

Express yourself with an attachment. You might excel at business, others may fail in their appearance, many might be talented and others will always be butter fingers, but we are all born inventors.

Go on, invent your shadow. Discover your genius towards an ethereal, enrapturing realm.

As I mentioned, I never imagined that I would get the opportunity to be a tourist.

Keep in mind that you are one too.